# TOM BLUEFOOT AND THE WESTWARD QUEST

## BOOK THREE IN THE "TOM BLUEFOOT TRILOGY"

Lloyd Harnishfeger
Pandora, Ohio

Order this book online at www.trafford.com
or email orders@trafford.com

Most Trafford titles are also available at major online book retailers.

Print information available on the last page.

ISBN: 978-1-4907-9303-0 (sc)
ISBN: 978-1-4907-9304-7 (e)

*Trafford rev. 01/08/2019*

www.trafford.com
**North America & international**
toll-free: 1 888 232 4444 (USA & Canada)
fax: 812 355 4082

For Lee Yoakam, a true friend.


In loving memory of Wes Yoakam
and Bob Harnishfeger

# BOOKS BY LLOYD HARNISHFEGER

HUNTERS OF THE BLACK SWAMP

PRISONER OF THE MOUND BUILDERS

COLLECTORS' GUIDE TOAMERICAN INDIAN ARTIFACTS

LISTENING GAMES FOR PRE-READERS

LISTENING GAMES FOR PRIMARY GRADES

LISTENING ACTIVITIES FOR MIDDLE GRADES

LISTENING ACTIVITIES FOR JUNIOR HIGH

THE KID WHO COULDN'T MISS

BLACK SWAMP WOLF

TOM BLUEFOOT, GENERAL "MAD ANTHONY" WAYNE, AND THE BATTLE
    OF FALLEN TIMBERS

TOM BLUEFOOT, CHIEF TECUMSEH, AND THE WAR OF 1812

TOM BLUEFOOT AND THE WESTWARD QUEST

TREASURE ON BEAVER ISLAND

HARRIET TUBMAN; CONVERSATIONS WITH AN AMERICAN HEROINE

# FOREWORD

"Tom Bluefoot and the Westward Quest" is a work of historical fiction. It is meant to enhance the reader's perception of the influence the fur trade had on development of the new nation.

Protagonist Toom-She-chi-Kwa [Tom Bluefoot] travels west of the Mississippi River in search of his friend, the escaped slave Simon Grant. The quest eventually leads him to join Manuel Lisa's fur trading expedition up the Missouri and its tributaries.

Known historical figures such as Manuel Lisa, John Jacob Astor, John Colter, and others are portrayed as accurately as research describes them. The various tribes and Native Americans, although necessarily somewhat fictionalized, are true to their geographical locations and the cultural aspects of that time.

It is hoped that this narration [book three of the "Tom Bluefoot Trilogy"] will provide an entertaining glimpse into this very significant period in our nation's history.

Lloyd Harnishfeger
Pandora, Ohio

Tom Bluefoot and the Westward Quest

Book Three

Tom Bluefoot tried to leap to his feet but his blanket tripped him up. Still half-entangled, he sat very still and listened . There it was again!

Moving one gray-streaked braid aside he cupped his ears and strained. The sound came softly. Like the sobs of a small child it send a shiver wriggling its way down his spine. Soundlessly he slid his threadbare blanket aside and eased his way to his feet.

In a single moccasin and taking small silent steps he advanced through the midnight darkness along the low bank of the Mississippi River.

The child sat scrunched up against the bole of an aspen tree, arms locked around her knees. Only the moonlight reflected from the calm waters made  her presence visible. Unmoving, Toom-She -chi- Kwa stared in abject astonishment. What was a young child doing here miles from the small village of St. Louis, the nearest vestige of civilization?

"Hello there." Tom said quietly.

"No! No, no no!" she screamed. "Let me alone! Oh, oh, oh..." The sobs came back, racking the small body as she attempted to pull a ragged older woman's garment over her eyes.

"Don't be afraid little one, I'll not harm thee."

"Keep away! She sobbed , struggling to stand. An injured leg was immediately apparent. Obviously hardly able to walk much less run, she scrabbled around until she was partially hidden behind the tree.

"Please," Tom whispered, "let me help you. I mean you no harm. Are you hurt? Thou must be cold as thou hast no blanket."

"You keep away I'm telling you. I can see well enough to tell you're an Indian man, even if you can talk like white folks. Just go away and let me alone. If I had a gun I'd shoot you dead, but I ain't got one so if you're fixing to kill me just do it,but don't do terrible things to me like Indians always do when they get somebody."

"I'm telling you I don't plan to hurt thee in any way. Furthermore I can help thee get warm, even give you something to eat if you're hungry."

"My Pa said, 'don't trust no Injuns no matter what they tell you'. He was right too. Now you listen to me, Redskin. I got three big brothers who all got guns and they're just off a little ways down river. They'll be here any minute, so if I was you I'd skedaddle while you still can. So there!"

"I certainly want no trouble from those big brothers of yours, so how would it suit you if I were to let you stay right here? You just sit right back down and I'll bring my blanket for you. Would that be alright?"

The girl made no reply as she sat back down, the injured leg thrust forward.

"I'll bet you're hungry. Would you like a piece of jerky to chew on until your brothers get here? Four of them you said, or was it five?"

"Four. It was four, and all of 'ems got guns. Big guns that shoot real straight too."

"Suppose I were to get you that blanket and a piece of jerky. Wouldn't that be a good idea for right now?"

"Then you'll sneak up and hit my head with those hatchets your kind always carry. No mister, you can keep your blanket and your jerky too. I'll just stay right here all covered up with Ma's dress. You go on back to your camp or whatever you've got. My brothers will be here any minute now."

"Very well. I'll let thee alone then. When I get back to my camp I think I'll make a small fire. I like a little heat on these chilly October nights. The firelight is nice too. It's not so scary all alone way out here in this wilderness when you've got a fire to sit by. Another good thing about a fire is it keeps the wild creatures away. Most of them are afraid of fire. Did you know that? Of course those four or five big brothers of thine wouldn't be afraid of bears and wolves and wildcats, what with their big guns and all."

"Why do you keep on talking and talking like that?"

"You are mighty lucky they are coming," Tom said mildly. "Of course they couldn't travel very well in the dark so they'll likely wait till morning so . . .." He looked up at the full moon for a second. "So it should only be four or five hours until they arrive. Good night then. Sleep well."

"Wait . . . I mean . . . just wait a little bit. What's your name anyway?"

"Toom-She-chi-Kwa."

"It sounds Indian."

"I reckon it does, since I am one. Most white folks just call me Tom. What's you name?"

She didn't reply. Her small body suddenly racked with sobs again.

Tom's knees popped as he struggled to stand. After a long look at her he parted the bushes and headed back toward his camp by the river. He pretended not to notice the child limping along behind him.

5

Still paying no attention to his guest, he quickly kindled a fire, cleared a small space, and motioned her to the fire near the heat.

"I got a stick here!" she suddenly growled, lifting a pitifully small branch. It was the only one she could get her hands on.

"Put the stick down. We'll need it for the fire later on. I'm glad you thought to bring it along." She flinched violently as he tossed the blanket toward her. "I didn't hear your name yet. I think I told you my name is Tom. Tom Bluefoot."

"Meg. I've still got this stick, and I think I hear my brothers coming along the river. They'll be here any minute, so you remember that mister! What's the matter with your arm?" she asked as she wrapped his blanket tightly around her. She didn't thank him.

"I got injured in a war. Here's a strip of jerky. Sorry there's no salt for it."

She snatched the meat, tore at it with her teeth, and gobbled a large piece.

"You better chew that good, Meg. It's mighty tough. Could give thee a belly-ache if it isn't chewed up good."

She was asleep, a string of jerked venison still hanging from the side of her mouth.

*

Toom-She-chi-Kwa woke with the dawn, Meg was still asleep, wrapped in the blanket. He blew on the coals to bring flame, threw on a few sticks, and slipped away with the water pan.

"Tom! Oh you Tom! Where are you at, Tom?"

"I'm coming Meg. Just dipped up some water to boil for our mush. Art thou hungry?" He arranged the pan on the fire.

"I've still got my . . .my . . .Where's my stick at, Indian?"

"It's on the fire. Just what we needed too. Are you cold?"

"Yes! I was too cold to sleep a bit last night. That was good too, since that way I could keep an eye on you. Why do you talk so funny?"

"Here girl. I've only got one spoon so you take a bite then I will. We'll take turns. Would that be alright with you?"

"This tastes awful! Don't you have any salt or sugar or anything? It's nothing like Mama makes. And no milk either. How can you eat this stuff? And I asked you a question about your talk. You ain't answered me. I thought Indian people said 'ugh' and 'me go' and like that."

"I don't mean to speak differently than others, but I was raised by a Quaker man. That's how they speak, so sometimes it just sort of comes out. Now I have a question for you, Meg. What are you doing out here all alone? Where is your family?"

The girl suddenly began to cry. "I don't . . .I . . .I . . . don't know *where* they are! I got lost in the woods. Daddy had me go after kindling. A big storm come up all to once and it got awful dark and . . . and . . . Oh, I don't even know where they are or where I am at neither. You ain't going to hurt me or scalp me or anything are you? Are you Tom?"

"Of course not! I'll not harm thee. As soon as we're through eating I'll help you find your family. Would that be a good idea do you think?"

"Oh *yes*! Yes it would! Let's start right now!"

"It's hardly light out yet, but we'll go very soon. What's wrong with your leg? Can you walk at all?"

"I was just so scared! The lightning and that terrible thunder. I thought I was running back to our wagon, but the more I ran the more I couldn't find my way."

"Didn't your brothers go looking for you? Surely you couldn't have gone far from camp."

The girl said nothing, but Tom noticed she was scraping diligently at the few remaining crumbs of the "terrible salt-less gruel"!

"That wasn't real honest truth, Indian Tom. See I only got one brother. He's six years old, Rodney is. So he couldn't do nothing to find me."

"I see. Didn't you shout for help? Perhaps they could have heard you."

"The storm! I yelled and yelled but they couldn't hear me for that awful thunder. I ran hard as I could but it was so dark I fell over stuff, and then I hurt my leg. This one here, see?"

Tom watched as she shoved a knee out from under the blanket. He studied her for a moment, then asked a question. "How long have you been lost Meg?"

"I think it's been two days. And two nights too. The nights were awful! Then I smelled some smoke and sneaked up and seen your fire. I tried to keep real quiet, but I kept bawling and you came and found me. I was scared of you."

"You're not scared of me now are you?"

"No. No I'm not. Not anymore. I think maybe . . . did you hear something just then?"

"No, I didn't hear anything. What did it sound . . ."

"Sh! Listen!"

"I'm sorry Meg, but I can't hear well anymore. Too many cannon shots and . . ."

"It's <u>Daddy</u>! Over here! I'm right here!"

"Meg? Megan, I'm <u>coming</u>!"

The man came crashing through the bushes at a dead run. His homespun clothing was in tatters, and dribbles of blood seeped from scratches across his arms. "Oh Meggie, honey, we was afraid you was lost forever. O thank God you're . . . you're . . . what's that Indian doing here?" He raised a battered fowling piece and pointed it at Tom's chest. "Redskin if you've harmed my little Megan I'll kill you right there!" he snarled. He pulled the girl under one arm but kept the gun steady.

Tom stared in terror at the crazed look on Megan's father's face. Having spent over nine years in various battles he well knew the threat of death when confronted with it. "Sir, I assure thee I have not harmed the child in any way. She stumbled onto my camp in the night, and . . ."

"That's enough out of you. Now shut your mouth. Even so you can speak good English I'll not hear another word!"

"Oh no, Papa! Mr. Indian Tom is a nice man. He never hurt me or scalped me or <u>nothing</u>! He gave me his blanket and some mush too. So don't be mean to him, <u>please</u>."

"You're too young to know about what can happen to girls who get caught by Indians."

"But Papa, he's been good. I was cold and scared and he made fire and cooked stuff and we shared his only spoon. So don't . . ."

"Be quiet girl. Alright I won't shoot him, but you and me are heading back right now. Your ma and little brother has been bawling their eyes out. They'll be mighty happy to see you. That's sure! Now throw that filthy blanket over to him and let's get going."

"But Pa, I got a hurt knee. See here? I can't walk so good, but I can go slow I think."

"Did he do that?" Jacob growled, starting to pull the weapon up again.

" No! Oh no he never! I fell over something in the dark. Maybe a log or a root."

"Was that Indian fooling around with that hurt knee? Maybe claimed he could cure it for you?"

"No he didn't." She turned to Tom and asked, "do you know how to fix a sore knee Tom? My Grandpa said Indian folks can heal hurts and things like that. Can you Tom?"

"I'm unable to do things like that. I'm sorry Meg, but  . . ."

"How'd you learn such good English? Probably from some white captive your kind had tied up somewheres. That it?"

"I was raised by a Quaker, the owner of a grist mill in Fort Pitt. It was the way he talked."

"A likely story. Come on Meggie, we're going to your mama and our wagon."

"Sir, I don't know thy name, but I would suggest that the child will only cause further injury should you attempt the long trek through the brush back to your camp. I have a suggestion should you care to hear it."

"She can walk good enough. I can see what you're planning and I don't like it!"

Even though he was not asked, Tom spoke up anyway. "Sir", he began politely, "may I ask thy name? It would facilitate our conversation immensely.

My real name is "Toom-She-chi-Kwa". It means 'he paints his foot'. Non-Indians usually just call me Tom."

"Listen to his fancy lingo. Who do you think you're foolin' anyway? You Injuns got more tricks than fleas on a old hound dog. Well Mr, Tom foot, I've had some schoolin' too. Near six years off and on, so you're not takin' me in!"

"Pa! Pa! I want to go to Rodney and Mama. Let's go! I can limp along if you don't go too fast. Tom, our name is Baker. Pa's Jake . . .er . . . Jacob, and you already know my name. Now Papa let' get goin!"

"Mr. baker, I have a suggestion. There's a game trail that roughly follows our eastern bank of the Mississippi. It would be much easier walking on that as you make your way south."

Jake said nothing, but with one beefy hand under his daughter's arm, started in the direction Tom had indicated.

"Are you coming Tom?" Megan shouted. "You come too. I want Momma and Rodney to see you."

"No he ain't coming," Jake said. "We've seen enough of that red devil. Come on."

"But Poppa, he's got a bad hurt arm from a war and . . . and . . . I think maybe he kept me from getting dead"

"I'll allow it then, but it's against my better judgment."

*

It was hot walking on this morning in October, 1816. Little Meg proved to be a determined walker, but it was obvious that her leg was giving her more and more trouble. Tom offered to help, but Jake hadn't allowed it. So the Indian stayed behind, saying nothing, his pack secured by a tumpline.

"Poppa look!" Megan suddenly shouted. "There's a little boat down there. It's coming this way."

"So it is, Meggie. You've got young eyes. Looks like two men in it. I'll see if they'll stop and talk. Maybe they can show us a better trail or something."

"I'll do the talking Mr. Baker," Tom said quietly. "Lay the gun on the ground and spread your arms wide. Do you have a sidearm?"

"You won't be doing no talking for <u>me</u> Injun. I can speak for . . ."

"Better do like he says Poppa. He knows how things are done way out here along the Mississippi River. We maybe don't."

The little group stood by the river's edge, both Tom and Jake's arms still spread wide. "Hello small craft!" Tom shouted. "We would be pleased to parlay for a moment."

"We're comin' in. Hold yer horses." The punt slid onto the muddy bank but neither man got out. "What in tarnation's goin' on here?" the larger man asked, spitting a stream of tobacco juice in their direction. "What's that Injun with you for? He your slave Mister?"

"Welcome travelers," Tom said. "This little girl got lost from her family. We're seeing that she gets back. Her father here is Jacob Miller. Their wagon is probably a day's travel south downriver."

"Why'd you take up with that halfbreed Baker?" He gave a great sigh. "You greenhorns don't know what you're in for out here in this country." He spat again and wiped his mouth on a greasy sleeve. "Come on Brady, we got to be getting' on north. Them beaver ain't gonna wait around for us to get out to the far country."

Tom spoke up. "As you can see, little Megan here has injured her knee. More walking may do serious harm to the joint."

"So what, Injun? There ain't nothing we can do about it. Get you pole and push us off, Joe."

"You gentlemen look like the type of men who would never abandon a white child in distress. Am I wrong in my assessment of your character?"

The two were obviously confused. It seemed like they had been paid a compliment but they didn't know the meaning of some of Toom-She-chi-

Kwa's words. "Wal now," Brady began, scratching his shaggy head, "wal that is . . . why shore we'd help the little gal, but what can <u>we</u> do?"

"Come on Pa. My leg feels better now. Let's get going again."

"Yes, we thank you men, but we should be on our way," said Jacob, drawing his daughter under his arm.

"You ought to rig up some kind of crutch for the kid," Brady finally said. "A forked stick would do it. Probly ought to pad it on the top so the girl don't get a gall from it."

"I have a favor to ask of you men if you have a minute to listen."

"Hey, we ain't doin' no favors for no thievin' varmint like you! We still ain't sure about just what you're doin' with these fine white folks anyway."

"The favor is not for me, it's to benefit Miss Megan Baker. She needs to get off her injured knee. If thou would be so kind as to turn thy craft around and head south she could ride along on your boat."

"Not atall Redskin! We got to get north. We hope to join up with Manuel Lisa before he and his men head west to the beaver trappin' country."

"Suppose we were to pay you for perhaps two days' interruption of your plans," Tom Bluefoot suggested.

"That might change our minds at that. You got any cash money, Injun?"

"None. But perhaps the Baker family could accommodate you travelers."

Jacob spoke up, but with obvious reluctance. "We've got a little Spanish silver left, but we were saving it for farm equipment and seed. How much would you charge to take us on?"

"Poppa, <u>Poppa</u>! I can walk some. Maybe you and Tom could make me a crutch like the man said. Don't spend our seed money just to get me back to our wagon!"

"You can be proud of your daughter," Tom said quietly.

"How much?" Meg's father asked miserably.

"Wal now, let me and Brady do some figurin' on this here since we had no idee of goin' back south and missin' mebbe two days hirin' on to old Lisa's beaver trappin' experdition, so . . . let's see . . ."

"Two dollars!" Brady said. "We're wasting time with all this palaver. That's a dollar a day. Silver money only. No greenbacks. Take it or leave it Baker."

"Very well. Her mother would want it that way. How soon can we get started?"

"Why right now! Climb in here little girl. You can set on that pack right there in the middle."

"Where do you want me to sit?" Jacob asked, casting a skeptical eye on the small boat.

"You? You ain't getting in here ! We're overloaded as it is. You can walk along the bank. Seein' as how it's fall, the old Mississippi is not running much faster than a man can walk, so you, Mr. Baker, will be hoofin' it back to your camp. Ought to be there by sundown." He glanced at Jacob, and with an exaggerated wink, said, "Unless we decide to just float clear on down to New Orleans. Old Madame Toucharay would likely pay plenty for the likes of this here youngun! Haw haw!"

"Oh no!" Megan wailed. "I don't want to go in the boat with these two men. I don't even know them, Poppa. I'll just walk like I said."

Tom stepped forward and confronted the boatmen. "I'll accompany the child," he stated emphatically. "that is if I have your agreement Mr. Baker."

"Now hold on! Hold on fer a minute. We could fit you in I reckon since you're no bigger than a flea, but we ain't about to 'commodate no thievin' Redskin in our boat!"

"It's that or lose two Spanish dollars, gentlemen," Toom-She-chi-Kwa said mildly. He dug into his pack and retrieved his only remaining firearm. "I would enjoy the boat ride and it will give me a chance to clean and reload my pistol."

The two men looked at each other. Jacob looked from Megan to Tom. Nothing was said for a moment, but then the girl limped forward and shyly placed her hand in that of the Indian, Toom-She-chi-Kwa, "he who paints his foot".

The rest of the day Tom and Megan drifted slowly southward on the sluggish Mississippi. Brady and Joe mostly slept except when the overloaded boat bumped a snag or encountered a sandbar. Meg had quickly learned to duck whenever Brady woke up and leaned over the side to spit. The slightest breeze was all it took to send the brownish goo flying her way!

During the long afternoon Megan continually coaxed the Indian to recount some of the adventures he'd lived during his forty-four years. With her leg propped up on the middle thwart she listened in awe.

Toom-She-chi-Kwa, abused by a drunken father, had at about age six been rescued by a kindly Pennsylvania mill owner. Eli, of the Quaker [Society of Friends] faith, taught the boy English, reading, and some basic arithmetic. All was well until some seven years later Tom's Wyandot father re-appeared and demanded his son back. From that time on, Tom once again lived with his Native American people.*

"That's when your arm got hurted like that?"

"Yes, Megan. An American soldier shot me, but that wasn't the worst thing that happened."

"It wasn't? What could be worse than that? Your arm's all . . . I mean . . . it's kind of skinny like ain't it? Does it hurt?"

"No, it doesn't hurt at all, but as thou can see I can't use it much. Look. Right there's where the bullet . . . "

"Oh Tom . . . don't . . . Oh I don't want to look at that little arm of yours! Oh, I'm sorry! That was rude. Momma learned me better than that."

"It's alright Megan."

"You said that getting shot in your arm wasn't the worst of it. What was the worser part?"

"My wife and two daughters were camp followers there at the battle.

*Read Lloyd Harnishfeger's first two books in the "Tom Bluefoot Trilogy; Tom Bluefoot, General "Mad Anthony" Wayne and the Battle of Fallen Timbers, and Tom Bluefoot, Chief Tecumseh, and The War of 1812.

The older girl, Tethica, saw me get wounded. She started running out of the woods toward her daddy and an American soldier shot her. She was just a little girl, about your age." He was quiet for a while, staring off at the trees along the shore.

"Look! There he is! See Tom? My daddy just came out on the bank again." She waved wildly and Jacob, obviously completely worn out, raised one weary arm in reply. Periodically the Indian trail along the bank veered inland. Jacob had no choice but to follow in order to avoid the thick growth at the river's edge, but most of the time he was in sight.

"What's your Pa doin' over there?" Brady asked, forgetting to spit.

"I think he's calling us in," Tom replied shading his eyes.

"Oh, lookee!" Meg cried, trying to stand. "See that big rock ? I remember that 'cause Rodney was sitting on it and fishing right there. Row us in, Brady! Hurry up! I'm home!"

Even before the boat had touched shore, Jacob waded in, lifted his daughter, and hurried on south, leaving Tom and the boatmen behind. Shouts erupted from inland as the family was reunited.

*　　*　　*

"Thankee kindly Miz Baker. It's been more than a coon's age since me and Joe had any real coffee. Kin I have a little more of that sow belly?"

Hester smiled as she scraped another thick slice of bacon onto his plate. "We are in  your debt Mr. Wales. And you as well Joe."

"Welcome Ma'am. Welcome I'm sure."

"Did you sleep well men?" Jacob asked kindly.

"We shorely did, Baker. How's that youngun of yourn getting on? Her leg still botherin' her I spect," Joe said, chewing on another bacon rind.

"Well," Jacob replied, "she's still sleeping in the wagon. Her Ma's seeing to her knee so I know she'll be just fine after a few days.

She's a tough little gal!"

Hester gathered the plates, saving the grease in a small tin can. "So you boys are planning to go after beaver fur are you? That must be difficult work. Dangerous too I suppose."

"Well Missus, we're shore plannin' on it, me and Joe is. But truth to tell we're hopin' to just trap on shares with Manuel Lisa's fur company till we can get us a stake good enough to start tradin' with the Indians on our own."

Joe belched mightily and remarked, "The real money ain't in trappin' and chasin' after critters. Trade with the Indians. That's how you get rich in the fur bidness."

"What all is involved in establishing a trading venture with the Redskins?" Jacob asked, looking from one to the other.

"It's simple enough Baker. You just buy a bunch of cheap bangles and doodads, lay 'em out on a blanket, and watch the red devils clammorin' to trade their furs."

Tom had been listening intently to this latest bit of conversation. He spoke up, looking from one to the other. "Do you and your brother know much about establishing a trading venture with my people?"

"He ain't my brother. I'd not claim him even if he was! Haw haw. No, he's a cousin of mine, Joe is. Anyway what's there to know about the fur trade? We'll do fine, and we'll make a big lots of money too!"

"You know the going price of a dozen double-barred crosses then?"

"Well . . . uh . . . not for certain sure we don't . . . not right now anyway," Joe stammered.

"And the Mandans," Toom-She-chi-Kwa persisted, "do they prefer plate or are they willing to accept the cheaper nickel silver?"

"Now that's about enough of that talk, Injun. I spose you <u>do</u> know all of that do ya?"

"What about the rate of exchange for Spanish silver and British coin? Will you accept scrip in your transactions? Have you purchased any castoreum*? If not you'll take few beaver."

*Castoreum, secreted from a scent gland at the beaver's tail, was an irresistible attraction for the animals.

"I said <u>that's</u> <u>enough</u>, Redskin!" Brady roared. "What are you trying to do anyway? Why you're nothin' but a skinny, one-armed, half-breed Injun, so don't pertend to lecture your betters."

"Gentlemen, <u>gentlemen</u>!" Hester cried. "Please don't shout, you'll wake our Meggie."

"Sorry Ma'am, but you can see how this here Injun has upset my cousin. And for no reason neither! We ain't bad sorts Baker. Shore we'll take a drink on occasion, and we been knowed to get in a scrap now and then, but mostly we're just simple folks as wants to make a honest living."

"Joe's right, Hester. We ain't bad fellers. I got a wife and two younguns back in Cramers Notch on the Ohiya. They're with my Pa and hisn till Joe and me gets back to 'em with enough money to buy some land. Now Joe here, he ain't never married so we got to find him a woman. Maybe we can fix him up with a squaw. If we can find a <u>clean</u> <u>one</u> that is. Haw, haw!"

Tom held his tongue. He didn't point out that Jake, Hester, and Rodney had discreetly positioned themselves <u>upwind</u> of the two odoriferous buckskin-clad cousins!

"I guess maybe I shouldn't of said that in front of him," he said nodding at Tom, but he didn't seem very sincere about it. "Anyway Toom-tom . . . or whatever you calls yourself, we didn't treat you nor the little one bad all day did we?"

"No you didn't, so I didn't have to shoot either one of you. Now I have a suggestion for you two businessmen. It's plain to see that you know little to nothing about the art of trade with the Natives. At the rate you're going you would soon lose all your goods and possibly your scalps as well. Also, If Manuel Lisa heard your plans he might not take lightly to the competition your venture would create."

"So what? I don't believe any of your smart-alecky words. If you are tellin' it true what could you do about it anyway?"

"It may be of interest for thou to know that I spent nearly two years as a helper and later the manager of Laveque's trading post in Green Ville, Ohio Territory. I speak the language of several Native American tribes, and can 'get by' in many others. Also . . ."

"Oh, pipe down Tom Foot. You're gettin' old. What do we care what you done way back then? Come on Joe let's get our gear together and shove off."

"I would be willing to join you in the fur business," Tom said quietly.

"You? Why we wouldn't take you on even if you was a white man,"Brady sniffed.

"Let me explain," Tom persisted. "I can figure the rates of the various coinage, interpret for you during the bargaining, help you select the best items for trade, and be certain that you don't intrude upon the complicated rituals followed by the different Septs you'll be dealing with."

Brady spit and wiped his lips. "I don't like it and I don't like you! Why would you want to do all this for Joe and me? What's in this for you?"

Tom studied the men for a moment then said, "I plan to go west of the river just as you do. I am attempting to find a friend who's gone out that way before me."

Jacob rose from the log where he'd been sitting and handed his breakfast dish to Hester. "How do you think you'll be able to find anyone west of the Mississippi? It's nothing but wilderness out there, or so I've been told."

"Yer right Jake. This here little Injun would have a mighty hard time of it way out there. Now Joe and me, weuns will do just fine. We're tough and smart, and we watch each other's back, Don't we Joe?"

"You bet yer boots we does, Cousin! Now Injun Tom, who's this here friend you're aimin' to find in all that wild country? Now Brady, we got to remember ol Bluefoot here is real well armed. He's got that fancy little pistol right handy in his pack. I reckon he could shoot his way outn any scrap as come his way! Haw haw!"

"Say now! Lookee here who's crawling out of the wagon," Jacob exclaimed."Meggie honey, you've been asleep a long time. Come to think of it, so have I! Here, let me lift you down. Who's that little tow-head back under the blankets? That couldn't be you brother could it?" Jacob teased.

"Ouch! Daddy my knee still hurts pretty much. Oh you're still here Tom. I'm glad! Momma, this Indian man has just done all sorts of things. He told us all about those old days while we were floating back down here in Brady and Joe's boat."

"Yeah he shore told us all about everything. Some of what he said might even be <u>true</u>. Haw haw!"

Hester poured a little more coffee into each cup, apologizing for the meager portion. "We're just about clear out," she said sadly. She gazed at the Indian for a minute, then asked, "What is your friend's name? The one you are trying to locate. Maybe we've heard something that would help. All the people we talked to on the trail out here from the Ohio Territory were glad to share any news they'd heard."

"Simon's his name, but he calls himself 'Dancer' these days," Toom-She-chi-Kwa answered.

"Momma! Remember back in that little town where we had to fix our wagon wheel? There was some Indian people off by that little crick where Rodney caught that big catfish. And it rained and rained so the trail was all muddy. Remember? Well a boy from the Carter wagon said there was a man doing a dance back in there. He got money for doing that. Anyway that's what the Carter boy said,"

"Yes, I do remember that. Here rest your leg on my knee. Does that feel better?"

Jacob gently set her foot down, then stood and dusted off his trousers. "I remember that too, but the Carters had gone down to see that Indian camp. The one doing the dancing couldn't be the one Tom here is looking for. They said he was a Negro man."

"That's <u>him</u>!" Tom gasped. "Do you know where he went from there?"

All the Bakers looked at each other, but shook their heads. "We never actually saw any of those Indians," Hester said, eyeing Tom carefully. "We're sorry, but . . ."

"It's alright. He always planned to go West, to the other side of the Mississippi. I may find him there. I know that any ferryman would remember him and his two Indian wives. I need to get north on the river, then check at every crossing place."

Rodney came climbing down from the wagon. "Did you know there was <u>pirates</u> on the river, Mr. Tom?" Rodney looked from one to the other. No one laughed. In fact the boy's father nodded sadly.

"The boy is right. You two men should be careful when you start north again. Just after we left St. Louis they were nailing handbills on trees and buildings. A one hundred dollar reward is offered for the capture of any members of the 'Blackstone gang'. According to an Alderman we met, there are three brothers. They hide along the shore till a small craft comes by, shoot the travelers, and steal all their valuables."

"We ain't skeered of no pirates," Joe declared. "Show him your gun, Brady."

The cousin ran off toward their boat. He was soon back, carrying a long buckskin bag. When he was sure all were watching he withdrew a beautiful long gun.

"Why young man," Jacob exclaimed, "that looks like a U.S. Model 1803 rifle! Where did you get such a fine weapon?"

"It's hisn!" Joe crowed. "That's the one he carried in the war against them Injuns as was always causin' trouble." He shot a look at Tom Bluefoot, but if the Indian was offended he gave no indication of it.

"Just let them river rats try something on Joe and me. I'll settle with them!" Brady bragged. "Come on Joe. We better get a move on. We need to be on the river and headin' north!"

"I'd like to accompany you." Tom's statement shocked them all.

"You? Why should we take you, Injun? You shore can't help us paddle, what with that shriveled up arm of yours."

"No I can't use a paddle anymore but I can help <u>pole</u> your boat north against the current. I watched men using that method on the Ohio River a month ago. It would give one of you a chance to rest while the other one and I kept on poling."

Joe liked the sound of some time to rest! "Might work Brady. If he don't do enough we can just throw him in the river."

"My oh my! You can't be serious," Hester said, carrying Megan to the wagon,

"We're serious alright. Well Indian Tom, your gear is still in the boat. Be in it soon as we're done here."

"Just a minute," Jacob Baker said. "Before you shove off I think you better hear what I've got to say about your plans."

"You?" Joe questioned him. "You ain't nothin' but a farmer. What do you think you can tell us about trappin' beaver and tradin' with the Injuns?"

"Better hear what Mr. Baker has to say boys. He's been here just north of St. Louis for almost a week. No doubt he's learned information that could be vital to us."

"Shut up Injun!" Joe snarled. "I was givin' serious thought to taking you with us, but it might be I'll change my mind. Ain't that right Brady?"

"Speak your piece Baker, but make it short. We need to be a-goin'."

"It's simply this. You plan to meet with Manuel Lisa don't you?"

"Well I reckon! That's about all we was talkin' about last night here in your camp," Joe said disgustedly.

"Well then you'd better get on the Missouri. That's the river Lisa and his company will take west."

Joe and Brady stared at each other in shock. Finally Brady demanded, "How do you know that, Baker?"

"I heard it too gentlemen," Hester stated calmly. "In fact several of Lisa's recruits passed through our camp just a few days ago. They told us they were heading for the entrance to the Missouri where other hunters and trappers were gathering prior to heading west to seek furs by trapping and trading with the Natives out there." It was a long speech for Mrs. Baker, but she knew their three visitors needed to know the truth. "Another thing," she continued, "how much do you really know about Mr. Manuel Lisa?"

"My oh my! You folks is just full of questions ain't you? Beggin' your pardon Ma'am, but we, Joe and me, we know he's about the biggest fur dealin' man there is. So what else do we need to know about him?"*

"I don't mean to intrude on your plans gentlemen, but as I'm sure you know, all of us out here on the frontier try to help each other as best we can."

"It's the truth for sure," Jacob said.

"Well not to be rude Ma'am, but get said what you're meanin' to! We've got to get goin' or we'll miss signin' on with Lisa and all of them."

"From what is said about him, at least what we've heard, he wasn't all that honest in his dealings. There's a very important family here name Chouteau. They had controlled the fur trade, and were said to be honest with their employees. He tried to take their business. Another thing is that Manuel Lisa was an adulterer!" Hester's outrage was apparent at this bit of news. "So you might wish to . . ."

"Hold on thar! Just you hold on! How can you, just a woman, get to know all of this about a real businessman?" Joe demanded.

Jacob gave a rare chuckle. "Joe, as an unmarried man you have a great deal to learn about women, especially women on the frontier! They talk to each other! Maybe you would call it gossip, but there's many a man, myself included, who've been saved from bad mistakes by learning to rely on what their women hear around campfires."

"Well maybe there's something to it, and I'm the first to say what I don't know about women would fill a book the size of old Webster's dictionary," Joe responded. "Still and all we got our plans all made. We wasn't borned yesterday neither, so Brady and me, we ain't about to get hornswoggled by nobody! Right Brady?"

*History is unclear regarding Manuel Lisa's place of birth. Some state that he was born in Cuba or one of the other Caribbean islands. For purposes of this narration, and because of a preponderance of evidence, New Orleans will be cited as his birthplace in 1772.

*There is no question of his parentage, being universally accepted as Christobal De Lisa and Maria Ignacia Lisa, or that he was raised and educated in New Orleans.*

*Well established in the fur trade by his early twenties, he had set up a more or less successful trading post in Indiana Territory. Later on he moved to the village of St. Louis at the juncture of the Mississippi and Missouri Rivers.*

*In 1796 he married the widowed Polly Chew, the mother of one daughter, Rachel. The union was blessed with two children. With their small family now well in hand, Polly and Manuel became increasingly fascinated by the fortunes being made by those entrepreneurs who organized fur-trading expeditions far into the unsettled Northwest.*

*One notable example was the Chouteau family, respected members of the St. Louis upper crust. Not in the least intimidated by their hold on the trade, Manuel Lisa set out to form his own company.*

*Fortune was with him as he encountered and befriended the famous explorers Merriwether Lewis and William Clark. Their return to St. Louis in 1806 with fascinating and almost unbelievable accounts of the abundant wildlife they'd encountered, was all Lisa needed. He formed his own fur company, and even persuaded Lewis and one of the Chocteaus to join with him.*

*Unfortunately Lisa was never very financially successful, even despite his "marriage" to Mittain, daughter of the Omaha Indian Chief. He and his men did, however, bring new knowledge to great areas of the unexplored far west.*

*Manuel's health was never good, following the strenuous and often dangerous forays into the wilderness. He died in St. Louis in August of the year 1820.*

*

"How far is the confluence from here?" Tom asked, as perplexed as the cousins.

"Only about three or four miles," Baker said. "You could float on down there in less than . . ."

"Pa! Pa! Lookee! Back in them trees!" Rodney's shouts alerted them all.

Megan stuck her head out of the wagon, her pointed finger confirming Rodney's words. "Those men all have guns pointed at us, and they're coming right into our camp!" she cried.

"Stay in the wagon children! Your father and I will see what the problem is."

"Don't move, any of you!" The man advanced, his rifle trained on Jacob Baker. Several other men then emerged from the forest, leading their horses. "I'm the sheriff of these parts. These here's my deputies." Over his shoulder he spoke to the others. "Looks like we got 'em boys. They're likely the river pirates we been huntin' for. I'll keep 'em covered. See what they got on 'em and in their packs on that boat."

"What's the meaning of this, Sheriff? These men are guests at my camp. They are merely travelers who plan to join with Manuel Lisa's trading venture."

"I also can vouch for them," Tom echoed. "I've been traveling with these men and they have proved to be nothing but upstanding citizens."

"Wal look at him!" One of the deputies snorted. "Looks like what we got here is a civilized Redskin. A fancy talker too. He's probably right in with them pirates. I ought to just put a bullet into the thievin' . . ."

"Hold on there Walt. I'll do the talking here. Go ahead and check them out. I'll keep an eye on him and this man and his woman too. Say . . . ain't you the ones that was living in your wagon just this side of St. Louis for a while?"

"We are indeed Sheriff. My wife and children are investigating land for homesteading. In fact we were present at your re-election rally just this past Thursday evening."

"So you was there was you? Will I get your vote? Haw haw!"

"Sorry, I can't vote yet, but when we get established you can be assured that you will be our choice for sheriff."

"You'd get my vote too, if we women ever get the right!" Hester growled under her breath.

"There's nothing suspicious on 'em or in their packs neither Sheriff," one of the men said, straightening up.

"Just as I said boys. There's no problem with these fine folks, nor that Indian neither." He tipped his hat to Mrs. Baker, shook hands with Jacob, and mounted up. "Now remember to vote for me just like you said. I'll say goodbye to you now. Keep an eye out for those pirates!"

Baker shook his head and grinned as the posse made its way south along the Mississippi. Politics out here near the growing village of St. Louis appeared little different from those he'd known in Virginia!

"Come on Joe. Them folks already told you they're about near out of coffee. Don't give him none Ma'am. He's had no decent raising so don't know no better than to wear out his welcome. Why he . . ."

His words were suddenly interrupted by a series of gunshots from the forest south of their camp. "Jacob! What's all that shooting mean?"

"I don't know, Hester, but might be the sheriff and his posse have cornered the river pirates that they've been . . ."

"I hear a rider coming this way fast," Brady hissed. "There he is. He's coming our way! Gimme my rifle, Joe!"

"It's back in the boat, Brady. I thought . . ."

"Hello the camp!" Without stopping to dismount, one of the deputies yelled a warning. "We run onto them pirates, but all three got away in the woods. They're still loose, and will probably be attackin' boats. So keep an eye peeled. Looks like they was headin' south though, so you folks should be safe enough. Gotta go! So long!"

Joe and Brady stared at each other in shock. They and Tom would be on their way in a matter of minutes, heading south!

\*     \*     \*

"The pack is too heavy for little Ona-give-Da ['Cattail]," Menseeta admonished. "She is but a girl."

"Little? You say <u>little</u>, Mon Cherie? She is taller than either of us. She must learn that what Phillipe say must be obeyed, the same as you. Now it is time to eat. Get some food ready while I smoke my pipe."

"How far, Phillipe?"

"Aha! Not far now. Crossing the 'Father of Waters' as your people call ze Mississippi, two days ago means only another two or three days ver' good march and we buy passage on ze bateau. No portaging for a week or more! Zen ze Missouri, she take us north and west."

"Oh it will be wonderful to be through with the walking and walking! These trade goods, they seem to get heavier with every passing mile. And, Phillipe, our little one seems to get heavier too!"

"Mother, put the cradle board on my back for a while. I can carry him and my pack as well. See how strong my arms have become," Ona-give-da said.

"After we eat perhaps. Now unload and gather a few more sticks for the fire."

"Phillipe, what is in these packs we all must carry? I know what the usual things are, but I would like to see what you are bringing for trade with my people."

"Why you not call me 'Dadee', or 'Pa-pa'? Always with you it is 'Phillipe this, and Phillipe that'. It is disrespectful to ze one who has taken you and your mother under my care."

"She means no disrespect, husband," Tadpole said soothingly. "It is only that Cattail remembers her real father, Toom-She-chi-Kwa, whom the whites call Tom Bluefoot."

"Zat man? Fie! He has been gone for . . . how long you say? Five year? Six? He is likely dead, or he has found a new woman in my country, Canada. Ze battles zey are over. <u>Done</u>! Ze war, she is lost to you Indians so why he come back to you anyway? A good man does not abandon his woman and child. Phillipe," he said pointedly to Cattail, "is your Pere now, Phillipe and no other!"

They had been on the march for nearly two weeks, following Indian trails westward from the Frenchman's home just across the St. Mary's River from Fort Detroit in Canada. He was short, muscular, and strong, having spent much of his early life as one in a team of "voyageurs" paddling the huge freight-carrying canoes across the wilderness to trade with the tribes living there.

After leaving his employment with the Hudson's Bay Company, he had decided to strike out on his own. There were fortunes to be made in the fur trade, and Phillipe Richeleau meant to make his!

"Why have you never allowed us to see any of the beautiful things we carry to the West, Phillipe? I mean Pa-Pa."

"Aha, Cattail, mon Cherie, after two more long days' march, zat will be 'four pipes', wife, if we are far from prying eyes I shall allow you and your mother to open ze beeg packs. Then you will see how it is that Phillipe will soon become ver' rich man!"

Two days later, camped at last on the eastern shore of the Missouri, the French would-be entrepreneur was true to his word. He spread his beautiful four point Hudson's Bay blanket on the ground and after yet another careful look around, began to extract examples of the precious trade items they had been carrying.

As Menseeta [Tadpole] repacked the cradle board with dried cattail fluff and fed her baby, Phillipe carefully took out each item. Circular silver brooches, which Tethica called "new moons", sparkled in the firelight.

The former voyageur placed each one carefully on the blanket. "Twelve of these beautiful things we have to trade,eh? Each will bring five prime castor skins."*

*Fur prices in the late seventeen hundreds had been very good, but as the number of animals declined, and the demand for furs decreased, the rate of exchange dropped dramatically. For example in 1765, Sir William Johnson's memorandum noting then current rates of exchange were: large knife-- one raccoon; pound of vermilion – two beaver; brass kettle – one beaver per pound of weight; silver arm band –three beaver; 1lb. gunpowder – one small beaver; gallon of rum – three beaver.

"Look at these!" his step-daughter cried, spilling the contents of a pouch onto the  blanket.

"Non! Non! Ma Cherie, only Phillipe handle the items for trade! You forget zis and I use ze switch on  you again, eh? You near growed up but not too much for ze stick!" His words were fierce, but she detected a flash of white teeth beneath his beard.

"What is 'castor'?"

"Now little one if you will learn to call me Pa-Pa' you may have one of these beeootiful ear-bobs for your self! Castor is the right name for ze beaver. Remember that!"

"You may call Phillipe whatever you like, Cattail. Yes you are nearly a grown woman now, but you must never forget your true father, Toom-She-chi-Kwa, Tom Bluefoot, no matter how many shiny things my new husband may give you,"

"But Mama, he is long dead! I can barely even remember what he looked like."

"He may be dead, but we are still unsure of that. Now you take care of your baby brother while I tend to the cooking pot."

"Watch your mouth woman!" Phillipe snapped, his voice low and menacing. "Don't forget that we are in a wild, wild country with no friend near us. Should you prove an unworthy and quarrelsome wife, then Phillipe and Cattail we abandon you and travel on alone! Phillipe has spoken!"

"Oh please Phil . . . I mean Pa-Pa', we must not quarrel. You have been good to us. We were almost starving until you arrived. Now let us be happy here in our camp. Show us more of what is so carefully wrapped in the large pack."

"Ver' well. Your words are wise, little one. Let us be happy indeed! Now see what lies within this pouch of otter skin." He untied the neck of the small bag and with a flourish emptied its contents next to the silver gorgets.

"Oh!" she whispered. "Beads! Many, many beads. They are so pretty! See, Mama, are they not the most beautiful things you have ever seen?"

"Yes!" Menseeta said, impressed in spite of herself. "When your true father, Tom Bluefoot, worked in Laveque's trading post back in Green Ville, he learned that the blue ones were the most valuable." Noting an angry look from Phillipe she quickly continued. "Was he correct in this, my husband?"

"Yes," Phillipe snapped. "Ze blue ones, they are ze best, but ze red, ze white, they make good trades too. You will see."

"Now look," the trader continued, unwrapping his treasures. There were silver medals, such as those struck by the Quakers, engraved with the head of George III, chest ornaments of various sizes, Hudson's Bay and American "peace medals", round gorgets, wampum, colored ribbons, knives, vermilion, arm bands, brooches,mirrors, and [unfortunately] a very small flagon of rum.

"When Phillipe done trading we be rich as old 'John Jake'* not so? Now light for me another pipe, Menseeta, then let us hear a story before we sleep. Daughter, is it not your turn? Tell us again of ze foolish thing you did when you were small."

"Oh, Pa-pa' you have heard that story before! It was the one I told when we waited for the boat to take us across the Oheeio, remember?"
"Maybe yes, maybe no. Tell it again."

The girl glanced at her mother who was trying to comfort little Castorelle. The baby was fussy on this cold October night. "Go ahead, my daughter. Your words may put this angry little one to sleep at last. Tell the story."

*John Jacob Astor, the richest man in America at this time. He had made his fortune in the fur trade.

\*    \*    \*

# CATTAIL'S TOTEM QUEST

"When boys are nearly grown up," she began, "they must spend days and nights alone in the forest. They do this to discover their special life guide called a 'totem'. Only boys are to do this, but I wanted to seek <u>my</u> totem as well. I was as strong as the boys, and a lot smarter than any of them!

Menseeta hung the cradle board from a low branch, set it gently swinging, and settled herself by the fire. "I told her it was a bad thing to do, but with her father gone to the war she did not listen to me. She was a stubborn child. She managed to get permission from Chief Mictaya, and walked into the forest without food or blanket."

I was not very hungry the first two days. I drank lots of water from the brook I was following. This helped some, but by the second night I was thinking only of food. There were berries nearly ripe but I didn't eat any. Part of the vision quest requires that no food be eaten.

On the fourth day I was beginning to feel faint. I wanted to lie down and sleep, even though I had slept through most of the night before. I kept walking. I believe it was the fifth day, or maybe the sixth that it happened. I had awakened on the bank of the stream when . . .

Cattail's voice was drowned out by the crying of baby Cas. "Aha," Phillipe cried. "Little Castorelle, he ver' strong voice! Just like his Papa. I was champion singer of our crew on ze beeg voyageur canoes. 'Phillipe, sing us on our way,' my companions zey would shout, and I, Phillipe, would oblige them. My songs would roll across the water as our paddles dipped in time. Now woman, take care of my son's needs. I am tired of his squalling. Now I wish to hear more about this girl's foolish attempt to be a <u>boy</u>! Ha ha!"

It was then that I heard it. Splash! Splash! Something was walking in the river. I got up and  . . ."

"Aha! Now the story gets better! It was a bear, not so? A beeg, beeg bear all shaggy and with teeth the size of a skinning knife, eh?"

"Stop it husband," Menseeta chided. "Do not make light of the girl's beliefs." Gently she rose and deposited little Cas back in the swinging cradle board. "Continue, my daughter."

No Pa-pa' It was not a bear, it was a bird. A crane. He looked at me and he <u>talked</u>!

"Oh <u>ho</u>! He talked did he? And what did ze crane say to a foolish little girl who wanted be a warrior like ze boys?"

"Phillipe, do you want to hear what happened or not? Cattail cannot continue if your voice keeps jumping in!"

Yes Pa-Pa', you will make me lose my place in the story. The crane asked what I was doing all alone in the forest. I told him I was seeking my totem. He speared a crawfish with his sharp bill, ate it, ruffled his feathers, and said, "You are a foolish girl, but a brave one. All this time you have been <u>looking</u>, but you did not <u>see!</u> I will be your totem. I, 'Gaya-ha', the crane." I looked around very carefully. Here was piece of crawfish shell, there a shiny stone exactly where the crane's foot had trod. Then, and this is the best part, just before he flew away down the river, the bird plucked a tiny feather from under his wing and dropped it in the water! I jumped in and grabbed it. I still have those three things in my medicine bundle. That is the end of my story."

"Cattail! Your real father, Toom-She-chi-Kwa, told us to destroy such little pouches as the one you wear on a cord around your neck! He said it was an evil thing that the white man's religion would not like! He would not have given you permission to go on that quest if he had not been gone to the war."

"It was a fine story, but it is plain that you simply imagined the whole thing. You were starving and when that happens strange things, zey can enter your head. Believe me, I, Phillipe, had such a thing one winter when our canoe was wrecked in the rapids and we spent months in the wilderness with hardly any food. No crane talked to me of course! Ha ha, Now go to sleep. It is late."

*    *    *

"Help, help! "My wife's baby is coming. We need to make a fire. We've no flint or fire striker. Come in! Please!"

"What should we do, Brady? We ain't got no time to go to shore again! We're likely to miss old Manuel Lisa's gang if we don't keep a-goin'."

"You're right Joe. IIerc's what we'll do; we'll pole in close to that woman and her man, but we won't go ashore. We'll throw them a fire striker or something and tell 'em we can't help with no baby bornin'. That won't take up much time."

"I would advise against you plan, Brady."

"Shut up Injun" Joe snarled. "Nobody asked you about it anyways."

Tom ignored the insult. As their boat continued drifting slowly south he tried again. "Did you notice how tall that lady is? And also, she was standing up there on the shore. And wrapped in a blanket too. Does that look like a woman about to give birth?"

"Maybe he's right Brady," Joe said. "Maybe . . ."

Tom bent forward and slid Brady's rifle across the center pack. "Get us closer and get ready with your gun, but keep it out of sight," Toom-She-chi-Kwa whispered. "Now tell them we're coming to help." He retrieved his pistol from the top of his pack where he always placed it.

"Hold on you two, we're comin' in," Brady shouted.

Tom continued using his good arm to pole their craft slowly toward the shore, the pistol clamped between his knees.

"This close enough?" Brady whispered.

"No! Get me in pistol range, you fool."

Joe started to stand up in the boat. "What is this? Them two is just . . ."

The 'woman' suddenly whipped off the blanket and as the 'baby' [a folded coat] fell to the ground. leveled a hidden rifle.

"Shoot him," Tom said, showing amazing calm. Brady's gun, slightly over-charged, roared and the man fell forward, his rifle blowing a harmless hole in the mud.

"Reload quick!" Tom hissed.

Paying little attention to his fallen companion, the second man scrabbled for the fallen rifle. Tom steadied his small pistol on one knee, took deliberate aim, and fired. A howl of pain and rage proved the shot had been effective but the bullet from such a small bore was not enough to bring him down.

"What's all this?" There was a roar, the bushes parted and a third man who'd been hiding, came charging onto the shore. He took in the situation at a glance, drew a huge pistol from his waistband and took aim. Brady, who had reloaded as Tom had told him, fired first. At nearly point-blank range the river pirate 'bushwhacker' was knocked backward, dead before he hit the ground.

"Get your rifle ready!" Tom hissed. "The man I shot is trying to pick up the pistol. You there on the shore," Tom yelled, "if you try another shot you will be dead!"
The man fell to a sitting position, one hand pressed against his side. "Don't shoot me mister," he whined, hardly able to speak. "I wasn't going to harm you. My brother made me do it."

Joe poled them in as Brady kept his rifle trained on the wounded man. "Get the guns Joe," Tom said, stepping ashore. "I think we've come across the river pirates the sheriff was hunting for."

"Now what? What we gonna do <u>now?</u>" Joe whimpered, putting both guns in the boat.

"There's a reward for these devils ain't there?" Brady asked of no one in particular. "I'll tell you what we're going to do. There ain't room in our boat for anybody else but we need to get him to St. Louis and claim that reward money. Got any ideas?"

"Tie him up good and get him aboard. I'll take the path along the river. I can run and I'll probably get to the village ahead of you. I'll find the sheriff and tell him to send some men back here to take care of the bodies."

"Don't let him, Brady!" Joe cried. "He's plannin' to get there ahead of us and claim the re-ward!"

"Shut up Joe! If you had half a brain in your head you'd know that you an me's got the only evidence; this here bloody pirate. Tom here has saved our bacon for us!" For the first time Brady had referred to the Indian as "Tom". It was said with respect. "Now," he continued, "get the rope and tie up this scoundrel. He's bleedin' a good bit on his side there, but it 'pears like he's a long way from dead. I'll load and prime all the guns, so there's no more surprises. Mister river pirate, you're gonna have a nice boat ride and before long they'll be holding a <u>party</u> for you. A 'necktie party' that is! Haw haw!"

"Hey there Tom Foot or whatever, looks like we're in your debt, Brady and me is. So no hard feelings is there?"

"That's right. I guess we don't know much about how things is done way out here. I think I can talk for my cousin when I ask if you're still willing to partner with us while we get rich, Right, Joe?" Politely he handed Tom his small pistol.

"Shore! Shore," Joe agreed, "But before we start out why don't we find these hombres' camp and see what else they got that we can use?"

Tom smiled as he adjusted his pack. "There's no need Joe. Remember, the sheriff saw them run off in the woods after the shooting back by the Bakers' wagon. They didn't have time to get anything."

"That's true Inj . . . er . . . Tom, true enough. And it's probably why they were so anxious to rob us this close to the village. They didn't have anything but their guns and the clothes on their backs. Well they won't be needin' <u>anything</u> now!"

Toom-She-chi-Kwa did indeed arrive ahead of those in the boat, but by the time he had located the sheriff [asleep in his tent] the others had tied up at the small dock. A crowd quickly formed and the cousins were hailed as heroes. Tom "just some old Injun" was ignored. The pirates had been a menace to river travel for too long.

Sheriff Tate strode up and immediately led a procession to one of the few log buildings in the town of St. Louis. "Somebody get the doc," he commanded, "We need to keep this scoundrel alive long enough to hang him proper. Anybody seen Mel? Melvyn Worth? I think he can identify this brute as one of them as kilt his wife and little daughter. I hear this hombre's two partners is beyond hangin'. Haw haw!"

A man in the crowd spoke up. "He ain't here no more sheriff. He was so broke up by what happened that he said he might just sign up with that Spaniard that's getting up a crop of men to go trappin'. Mel said everything around here just reminds him of his woman and child. Also those river rats stole near all he owned when they attacked his canoe. He'll go west with old Lisa if they'll have him. Says he can doctor them as might need it on the trip, even though he ain't no trapper."

"Anybody else gonna sign up with Lisa?"

"We are sheriff, just as soon as we collect our reward. We'll tell this Melvyn feller to report to you. If we can find him that is." Brady stepped up to Sheriff Tate and continued. "How soon can we get that hundred dollars sir? We figure Lisa's not gonna be here much longer. We plan to be on that river boat too when he leaves for the fur country."

"Reward . . . um . . well yes . . . of course," Tate hedged. "I've been speculatin' on that there too. Seems to me that me and my posse deserve some of that money since we're the ones as flushed them outn the woods so you three . . ."

"Now just a durn <u>minute</u>!" Brady exploded. "We caught them even when they tried to kill us. That reward money is ours by right." he looked around at the crowd, expecting agreement. Several nodded, but not many. It didn't pay to get on the wrong foot with the local sheriff!

35

Not willing to lose a single vote in the coming election, Tate clapped Brady on the back and made a suggestion. "Looks like we-uns both got a claim on that money. Maybe take a lawyer to straighten it all out. Now Judge Huston should be comin' around here on his circuit in a week or two. How about we just let him decide?"

Several in the crowd nudged each other. The sheriff was no dummy. He knew there was no way Tom and the cousins could wait around that long, and he rightly assumed that they had no money for a lawyer anyway.

Tom started walking back toward the dock, motioning Brady and Joe to follow.

Shortly before sundown Tom, Brady, and Joe approached the small table where Manuel Lisa was seated, still taking the names of those who wished to join his fur company. He took a long pull on the slim cigar he held. "Well, well," he said. "This is remarkable. Each one of you can write his name, even this skinny little Indian! It will be pleasant to have some educated trappers on our little journey. And you, Tom is it? I appreciate that you have met with some considerable misfortunes in your life. I do not wish to be rude, but what do you think you can contribute to our cause, as it is obvious that you do not have the use of your left arm."

"You are correct in that assumption Senior Lisa. Actually I have no intention of engaging in the capture of the fur-bearers you seek. However . . ."

"Aha! Your speech and manners are beyond reproach. Please continue."

"I speak English, some Spanish, and several native languages and their dialects. Having lived with my Wyandot father and his sister in Chief Tecumseh's village, I am well-versed in the often complicated beliefs and rituals of my people."

"My oh my!" Lisa remarked sarcastically, "Anything else?" Several of the buckskin-clad men nearby laughed aloud.

"Yes. I spent two years working in the Frenchman Leveque's trading post in Green Ville, Ohio Territory. I can read, write, and cipher. It is my sincere belief that even a one-armed man can be of much service in your endeavor."

Lisa's white teeth flashed in a slight smile. "Very well compadre, we'll give you a try. Get your gear and climb aboard."

"There is one more thing I should tell you," Tom said.

"I might have known! What is it, Indian Tom?"

"I wish to be perfectly honest. I have no intention of engaging in trapping beaver. I'm trying to go west to find a friend who has gone west before. Should I get news of him I will be leaving your fur company."

"Well said." He glanced around at the noisy, unkempt men around them. "It will be a pleasure to have at least one honest man accompanying us. You may depart should you obtain news of your friend. Now for your first assignment: tell these drunken louts that I am not of Spanish descent. Born and raised in New Orleans, no less, I am an American!"

For some time Tom had been noticing a tall, skinny Indian intently watching him. Dressed in dirty white man's clothing, the brave sidled near. "You know I. Know huh! Me Charlie . . . you Toma."

"You know me? I don't remember you . . ."

"Si! Know I. Fort Dtroit. You speak for Britty Red-Coats! Ha!"

"You were at the surrender of Fort Detroit?"

"Genral Hull. A old one. Huh! Fraid . . fraid! . . . no fight. Fraid!"

"Yes, he was too old and sick to defend the fort. I felt . . ."

"See, see Charlie knife? I make it! Me!"

The small knife was thin and deadly-looking, nothing like the big "Bowie knives" carried by many of the men in Lisa's company. Charlie jabbed a dirty finger in Tom's chest, leaned forward and said, "Boss Lisa, he call me Charlie the terperter," he hissed. "Indian Tom, you remember!" He drew a finger across Tom's throat, held the stiletto near Tom's eye, and scuttled away.

*         *         *

"Ze boat ride, she mighty nice, eh? How you like Menseeta? Cattail? Phillipe he sees to it we get to ze Mandan village the easy way, not so?"

"It was fine, husband. Little Castorelle liked it too. So many boats on this Missouri then, but not now. We must be far to the north and west. Will you ever be able to find our way back, Phillipe?"

"Ha ha! Phillipe he was called 'pathfinder' by the other voyageurs. I find our way home,  you bet! And with sacks of silver money too!"

Cattail stirred the fire and replaced the pan of tea. "Silver, Phill . . . I mean Pa-pa'? I thought we would be bringing back hides and pelts."

"Mon Cherie, you are a smart one. I always say zat girl tall, slim, like ze willow. Beeootyful! And smart. Ver' smart! Is it not so, woman?"

His wife did not have time to answer, for two Mandan braves suddenly appeared, their approach silent as the flight of an owl. Phillipe motioned that Menseeta should welcome their visitors.

"Trade? You come to trade with us?" she said, using a sort of combination Algonquin, Mandan, and sign language.

"Trade!" the oldest and obvious leader of the two grunted. "Soogar! Soogar-tea!"

"What does ze savage say?" Phillipe whispered.

"He is speaking English. My man Tom taught us that language. He says he wants  tea with lots of sugar in it."

"Shall I get some more sugar from my pack Pa-Pa'?"

"Non! Non! First we see what furs they have."

"But they don't have any, Phillipe."

"Ah but zey do, wife! The women, they will be carrying the peltries. The men they catch the animals, but that is all they do! The women do the ze skinning, tanning, and ze carrying. Take a lesson from that, woman!"

One of the Mandans turned and spoke a few words. Three women, each carrying a bundle of furs, entered Phillipe's camp. They stood very still, their features accented by the firelight.

"Soogar-tea!" The leader demanded again, thumping the butt of his lance on the ground mere inches from the girl's foot. He sat down, casting baleful glances at each of the traders.

"Get the sugar, daughter," her mother said quietly. "Get the kettle boiling, Two pinches of tea, but a full ladle of sugar."

"Spread my capote here by the fire. Do not hurry." Phillipe nodded and smiled at the Indian women, gesturing that they should spread the furs on his garment. "Sing a little song for them Cattail! Be happy!"

"But what should I sing, Pa-Pa'? I don't have any . . ."

"Just sing anything or hum a little. Make zem think this is a little party, non? We are ze good friends here, not so?"

"I will get cups, Phillipe."

"Non! No cups. These 'children of the forest' will no doubt drink right from the kettle. Now wife, hand the kettle to the one who does the talking."

"But husband, it is almost boiling. Too hot to drink."

"Do as I tell you. You will see."

The leader seized the kettle, slupped noisily and passed it to his companion. Only after both men had taken several turns were the women given opportunity to drink a little "soogar-tea".They smiled shyly at each other, then exchanged a few words that neither Phillipe nor Menseeta could understand. They handed the vessel back to the men who quickly finished the sweet brew.

"O-te-Ha!" the leader said. He smacked his lips and made a grand gesture at the truly beautiful pile of furs. Phillipe and his step-daughter knelt by the pelts, their faces knit with frowns and what they hoped looked like disappointment.

"Non, non!" Phillipe murmured. He turned to Cattail, shook his head nd tossed a beautiful pine marten fur back on the pile. The girl added to the charade with an exaggerated sigh and look of disgust. Phillipe had trained her well in the art of barter!

They had been making slow progress northward for several weeks satisfied that their collection of pelts would bring good prices when they returned to Detroit. Both the Oto and Mandan had welcomed them, but Phillipe was not satisfied with the trades they had made, since the natives had no silver money with which to buy his trade items.

The principal negotiator for the natives, whose name they had learned was ge-ye-dakwa ["Stone Hammer"] or Marteau in French, locked eyes with

Phillipe. A sardonic smile curled one side of his lip. As a Mandan whose people had been dealing with traders ever since their contact with Lewis and Clark, he and his companions were only amused at such awkward machinations. He picked up the marten skin, blew gently on the silky fur to prove its quality, and shoved it back at the Frenchman.

"What he say?"

"I did not understand much of that," Menseeta admitted, "but mostly I think he was telling us that he was no fool, and had been dealing with traders like us many times before! He was using some English."

The other Mandan now uttered a rapid flow of words. "This time, Pa-Pa', he keeps saying 'Lisa, Lisa'. I think he is trying to tell us the great man, Manuel Lisa, is here, in their village! That man may give better silver than we do."

"Manuel Lisa is here?" Phillipe gasped. "Maybe that is not what he meant, or maybe he lies. Not so?"

Menseeta spoke up then, careful to keep her voice calm and easy. "I don't think he is lying. In fact I know he is telling the truth.

The Mandan girl who came to our camp this morning to trade berries for a brooch told me!"

"Mon Dieu!" the Frenchman roared, not caring if the Indian men understood him or not. "Why you not tell me zis, woman?" His wife Menseeta made no reply.

"So! Now we must make ze best barter that we can. Maybe we not get as many pelts as Phillipe like, but since we know that the Spanish charlatan is here, we be more clever! Not so?"

His daughter hid a smile behind a beaver pelt and said, "Pa-Pa' we'd better not try to fool these people again. They seem to know more about trading than we do!"

"Pah! Nobody knows more about ze trade zan me, Phillipe!
But maybe you are right. Throw some pine cones on the fire. That will make the silver shine! Ze women will want what we have to offer."

Phillipe's wife and step-daughter worked quickly, arranging a selection of silver brooches, ear bobs, and double-barred crosses on a square of bleached doeskin.

The women crowded close, speaking softly to each other as they examined each item.

The trading went on for some time. The fire had been replenished twice before all the transactions were finally completed. Both parties thought they had made the better trade, so there were smiles and hand shakes all around.

After a final pan of "soogar-tea" had been consumed by the Mandan visitors the traders rolled up in their robes, satisfied that the encounter had been successful.

Shortly before dawn when the Frenchman and his family were sleeping soundly, the two braves slipped back into the camp. The fire had long since gone out but the moonlight was strong enough for them to ease the pack of furs from its resting place between the trader and his wife. Not satisfied with the pelts however, they also attempted to steal the bag of remaining trade goods.

There was a tinkling sound.

"Huh? What you . . ."

"Stop!" Menseeta screamed, punching her husband. "They are stealing <u>our goods</u>!" Still sitting she instantly locked her arms around the legs of the nearest Mandan. Phillipe, wide awake now, raised the knife he always kept by his hand when he slept. Before he could strike however, Stone Hammer whipped an arm about the trader's neck. A struggle ensued, the moonlight hardly enough to tell who was fighting whom!

The Mandans had forgotten Cattail. Quick as a cat she sat up and felt for a weapon. Her fingers fell on the razor-sharp tip of an arrow they used as a sample. Fearing that her Pa-Pa' was in imminent danger of strangulation, she did not hesitate. With all her young strength she thrust the arrow into Stone Hammer's thigh. He reeled back, released his arm, and scrabbled away into the brush. The other Mandan was already disappearing into the forest, carrying the entire bag of furs. Pursuit would have been useless.

The morning sun fell upon a sad and angry threesome. "We are ruined!" Menseeta groaned. "Ruined and with no way to buy our way back to Detroyet. Or anywhere else!"

"No my pet! Phillipe never give up. You will see. You are fine wife. Lucky for us you heard ze thieves trying to take everything. Let zem have ze furs. We still have many pieces to trade. Maybe we go see this Lisa. Maybe he help us get our furs back."

"Oh Pa-Pa', what if that man is angry with us? He might not like anyone else trading right where he is."

"Maybe yes, maybe no, my pet. Phillipe he make up his mind and then it is done! While other men, they sit by the fire and try to decide what to do, me I already gone half a day march, eh? Ha ha!"

"Let us eat a little now," his wife, Menseeta, spoke up.

"Good. We eat, zen we find this great man who everybody say is so smart. I soon show him how we, ze French traders, do things. Cattail, get ze packs ready. We go as soon as ze sun she a little higher."*

\*            \*            \*

"Oh, Pa-Pa'! Look, there are houses everywhere! More than five double hands maybe. So <u>many</u>!"

"Get back, filthy flea-bitten cur, or Phillipe kick you!" The dog did not stop his stiff-legged snarling approach.

*\*The large and well situated Mandan tribe lived in round, permanent structures made mainly of arching poles covered with packed earth. Like many Native Americans prior to contact with the Europeans they were a very religious people.*

*Near neighbors, the Hidatsas and Arikaras were generally at peace with the powerful Mandans, and some trading among the three tribes took place from time to time.*

A boy of perhaps ten winters came running. He grabbed the dog by a hind leg, held him back, and smiled at the three strangers. He spoke a few words in the Mandan language which they could not understand.

"Give ze boy a fishhook," Phillipe said. "See if you can make him lead us to the great Manuel Lisa."

The lad's eyes bugged in surprise as Cattail dangled the prize object near his hand. "Leezia?" she asked. "Manuel Lizia?"

"Lisa! Lisa!" he answered, reaching for the fishhook.

She drew it back.

"Leeza?" she asked again. She pointed in each of the directions with a questioning look. Understanding at last he jabbed a finger to the west and said "Lisa!"

Cattail handed the object over, turned his small head in the direction he had indicated, and gave him a gentle push.

Holding the steel fishhook high for all to see he marched proudly forward, Phillipe, Menseeta, and their daughter staying close.

Tethica and Menseeta began lagging behind, taking every opportunity to smile at the Mandan women who were busy at their chores. They hoped to be invited to enter one of the huge, dome-shaped lodges. Like women everywhere they were curious about these elaborate, permanent structures, what they were like inside, and how the people lived in them. They were mostly ignored until Cattail slipped one earring off and handed it out toward a gray-haired woman. Shyly she smiled, took the bauble and indicated that they were welcome to enter.

Tethica [Cattail] kept staring at her. What was it that was so different? Something about her eyes. They were <u>blue</u>!* Blue like some of those she had seen in the Americans in the army of the "Mad General", Anthony Wayne.

*Rumors of "blue-eyed Indians' among the Mandan can be corroborated. Several theories regarding how this came to be, such as Viking explorers intermarrying with the natives, have been largely proven untrue by the new knowledge of genetics. Another persistent legend claims that a Welsh prince named Madoc [a real person] made contact with the Mandan in the thirteen hundreds. Many scholars continue to believe that early contact did occur, and that light-skinned Native Americans was the result.

The tour was suddenly interrupted by a younger woman shouting into the lodge. She continued jabbering excitedly in their language until their hostess practically pushed them outside. People were rushing along between the lodges, heading out of the village to the west.

They came shoving and crowding into Manuel Lisa's encampment. Menseeta, with little Castorelle in the cradle board on her back, was the first to see her husband engaged in a fight with a Mandan brave. Cattail saw the action too. "Pa-pa'!" she screamed. "Pa-pa'!"

A crowd of noisy, half-drunk trappers had ringed the fighters and were urging them on. Phillipe was holding his skinning knife low and forward as the two circled each other. The Mandan was also armed. He held a tomahawk in his right hand, a scalping knife in his left. It appeared that as yet no blood had been shed.

The daughter started to run into the circle but her mother grabbed her arm. "Do not go near them! You could be cut, or if you distract Phillipe for even a second he will be killed!"

Exactly at that moment a handsome, black-haired man strode directly into the fray. With astonishing courage he positioned himself directly between the furious combatants. "What is all this?" he demanded in perfect French. "I will not have members of my organization, be they red or white, complicating the pursuit of our fortunes. You", he growled, facing Phillipe almost nose-to-nose, "who are you? I don't remember you signing on as a member of our expedition."

The Indian thrust himself forward and began a rapid volley in his own language. Lisa silenced him with a contemptuous look and turned to Phillipe. "Put that knife away you fool. This man could cut you into small pieces before you could take two more steps. Now I ask again, who are you and what are you doing here in my camp?"

Upon hearing the French language, Phillipe exhibited enormous relief. He answered quickly.

"You are Manuel Lisa, are you not?" he began courteously. "I was eleven years a voyageur for the Hudson's Bay Company. Last year I decided to become a trader on my own. My wife, daughter, and I have been trading since the spring and I apologize for . . . for . . . for intruding on your territory. I didn't know . . ."

"Forget that!" Manuel Lisa broke in. "Never in your lifetime could you be any kind of a threat to our trading successes!"

A great shout of laughter and some cheers erupted from the listening crowd of trappers. "Now what is this altercation about?"

The Mandan, having understood none of the French language exchange, again shouted out in the Mandan tongue.

"Is there one here who can translate for this man?" Phillipe's daughter hurried up.

"I can do eet," she stated proudly.

"And who is this perfectly lovely young maiden?" Lisa asked, obviously taken with the beauty and poise of the sixteen year old girl before him.

"Ah, Monsiuer Lisa, she is my daughter. Next to her stands my wife with our baby son, Castorelle."

"Very well. What has this Mandan been saying?"

"He say, monsieur, that this man, who is Phillipe, my pere, try steal he furs. That be a full lie. He lie! Oui! A lie, and . . ."

"Thank you young lady. Now Phillipe, tell me your version of what happened."

Before Phillipe could begin, a white man bustled up and spoke quietly in the Indian's ear. "Now," the man said, "this Mandan brave has an interpreter on his side. I will tell him everything you," he jabbed Phillipe on the chest, "will be telling our leader, Mr. Lisa. So be sure you speak the truth."

Manuel listened as the French trader described last night's attack and subsequent theft of the bartered furs.

Without a moment's pause the interpreter countered with an entirely different tale, one which claimed that Phillipe and his family were the true thieves who had stolen their trade goods and cheated the Mandans as well as their women!

Manuel Lisa stood by, arms folded, a slight smile playing about his black mustache. At last he spoke. "Well, well, we seem to have conflicting stories. Do either of you have any proof of theses accusations?" Although both declared their innocence there was actually nothing either of them could produce in the way of evidence, so without hesitation the leader rendered a verdict.

"Since it appears that the Mandan has the furs in question, and there being no way to resolve the issue, he will keep the pelts and we will get on with our trading until . . ."

"There be a . . a . . . evdences!" Cattail's somewhat broken French declaration shocked the crowd. This Indian, a woman at that, would dare to speak up right before their Captain? It was unthinkable! But Lisa surprised them even more. "Come here, little one," he said, observing her stately walk and pleasing form. "Stand by me. Speak slowly. How can you prove that the brave is lying?"

"While them fighted in white moon, I take . . . me taken . . . arrow with trade point, . . . metal iron <u>sharp</u>! Sticken leg! Him that. Leg sticken!"

"That's right Captain Lisa! She stick him good! She grab ze arrow we had fixed up with point of iron for ze trade. Ask him."

Lisa placed an arm around the trembling girl. "Grab him!" he shouted as the Mandan attempted to slink away.

"He say that be a lie by white Frenchman," the interpreter said. "He say no <u>woman</u> could ever wound him! He say white man liar, thief, and . . ."

"Enough!" Lisa growled. "Come closer. Why are you wearing leggings? Most of your men are in breech cloths only. Let me see!"

The man tried to walk away but several trappers grabbed him. One of them yanked the Indian's leggings down. The puncture wound was plain to see. Also evident was the exit wound where the arrow had been pushed on through in order to extract it.

"So it is true! You men get this man back to his camp. Find what peltrie is still there and give it back to this honest trader and his beautiful daughter." He still stood with an arm firmly around Tethica's shoulders.

"What is your name, Ma Petite?" he asked.

"I be . . . am . . . Ono-give-da am. I go to Pa-Pa' now go I."

"Oh no my dear. You must come to my tent. You deserve a reward for your bravery. I have much fine food, blankets, silver things . . ."

"But Mama too – Pa-Pa' too come they with?"

"Why of course! Of course." He somewhat reluctantly motioned to her parents, and even ordered a young Mandan woman to carry the cradle board.

Lisa's tent was large but not elaborate, designed for ease of packing and travel, the few furnishings were adequate, but only utilitarian. A center folding table was a different matter however. With a white tablecloth and real chairs in place, it rivaled those which might be seen in the few better homes being built in St. Louis.

Manuel motioned to an Indian woman who was waiting near the tent door. After a few words of instruction she departed to bring food and wine.

"Sit please. No, no. Not on the floor, here at the table. Now little one, what is your name again?"

"My real . . . my . . . I . . . real one Pa-Pa name is Toom-She-chi-Kwa. This one . . . here . . . new Pa-Pa' name Phillipe of." She hid her face in embarrassment at her poor attempts to speak to him in French. Actually due to her step-father's patient tutelage she could do better, but all the excitement had left her stammering like a child. "Real Pa-Pa named me Ono-give-da. White people name for I be 'Cattail'."

Lisa grinned and asked, "how did you get a name like that?"

Menseeta answered for her. "She take so many cattail fluffs to soak up pee-pee in cradle board Tom Bluefoot, her real Pa-Pa, him say 'that her name then; Cattail!'"

"And you sir are named Phillipe?" the expedition leader asked showing only polite interest. "And how do you,your wife and step-daughter find yourselves here in the Mandan village?" To the surprise of all the Captain had spoken in English.

Phillipe wriggled about for a moment, unused to sitting on a hard chair. "I, Phillipe," he said, trying to appear impressive, "was one of ze voyageurs. Many year I paddle ze beeg canoes for Hudson's Bay Company. We follow the streams, ze riviers, ze lakes, far, far to ze west."

For the first time Lisa took notice. "Do you remember the names of any of the western waterways you traveled?"

"Oui! Ze Platte, ze Powdaire, ze Yellowrocks. Ah, so."

"And the tribes in these environs, do you recall any of them as well?"

"Phillipe, he and sixteen other paddlers, we spend many happy hours in lodges of Arikara, Crow, Blackfooted. Nevair in my life such food! Buffler hump, tongue, livair sprinkled with gall, ducks, swans . . ."

"What are your plans now, Phillipe?" Lisa cut in.

"Trade! We trade like before. Pardon my bad manners. We thank you for getting our furs back. We still have much trade silver. We may still do well."

"I'm happy that the villain and his brother were apprehended before they could abscond with your furs. Are they all there?"

"Nearly all, Monseur. Again we say thank you . . ."

"Would you and your wife and daughter be interested in joining our trading venture? If so I will buy your remaining furs and your silver. At a profit for you of course." Even as he spoke it seemed that he could not take his eyes off young Cattail.

Phillipe was stunned, but after a moment he replied to the offer. "Kind! Kind!" he stated hesitantly, "but Phillipe, he want to be rich man in trade business. We do not . . ."

"We join you at right now !" Menseeta declared, glowering at her husband.

"Oui. We alright join up now." Phillipe, with a shrug of his shoulders, and a look of surrender, nodded to the expedition leader.

"When ze one who cooks ze meals, who can argue with zem, eh?"

"What about you, pretty one? Do you agree to accompany our little venture?"

Cattail turned a confused glance at her mother and step-father. Phillipe was smiling his approval. "But of what me do to be help? I not much know . . ."

"Do not worry. You will be of <u>much</u> help to <u>me</u>! Yes indeed! You say your name is Cattail?"

"Oui. My name mean 'Cattail' in white men talk."

"Not <u>anymore</u>!" Lisa stated emphatically. "You are much too pretty for [he grimaced] 'Cattail'. From now on you will be called Floret *Faeuri,* 'Forest Flower'." He shouted something in the Mandan language and in a few minutes food was being brought in. "Now we eat!" he said with a flashing smile. "Here, Floret Fleur, move your chair closer to mine." At this Menseeta nudged her husband, a look of anger and concern clouding her features.

As they finished eating, Lisa smiled at all three again. "Now I must meet the headmen to begin the trading. Phillipe, you and your wife will be welcome in Mr. Kaple's tent. Floret, there is lots of room in my tent for you."

Menseeta, now truly alarmed, was about to speak when Phillipe yanked her roughly out the door.

48

    \*        \*        \*

"Well," Joe grunted, trudging along the deck for what seemed like the millionth time, "these push-poles . . . ain't getting no lighter . . . are they Brady?"

"Save your breath, cousin. We got probably two more hours . . . to go yet, pushin' this old tub . . . agin' the current. Your shoulders achin' you bad agin' this morning?"

"I'll say they're bad! Do you 'spose our boss . . . on this boat would allow me to quit for a while?"

Conversation was difficult at best. Two men constantly walked the deck up and down on each side of "Captain" Lisa's last two keelboats. The lead boat had gone on before, all three being poled ever northward toward what the expedition members hoped would lead to trading success with the natives.

"How come we was told . . . to tie up them two days? Why Brady, . . . we're way behind Lisa's main boat by now. The Captain's boat . . . must be a hunnert miles upriver by now. What do you figger . . . is the reason for that?"

"I told you . . . to save your breath Joe. Nobody's . . . gonna relieve us till our shift's over. So just think about something else . . . and keep a-walkin' and a-polin."

"Look at our 'boat boss' over there . . . He's just settin' on that keg . . . and watchin' the land roll on by. Makes a body wish . . . he'd never heard of the Missouri River! When I get a chance . . . I'm gonna tell that smart alec . . ."

"No you won't neither! He's just doin' his job same as we are. And stop . . . talkin' bad about Tom Bluefoot. Lisa likes him . . . and that's one reason he took us on late like we was. That little one-armed Injun . . . can be just about the best friend we got on this trip . . . He went on the first boat with Lisa and them others . . . way ahead of us. So just keep that . . . in your mind, if you've got one!"

There is little wonder that Joe's shoulders were causing him pain. Manuel Lisa's fur company had been on the river for nearly two weeks, the current against them all the way. The only relief for the impromptu boatmen was the few occasions when a good south breeze filled the crude sails erected on each of the boats. Brief respite from poling also came occasionally when one of the ships hit a snag or grounded on one of the ever-shifting sand bars. Welcome as it was, the two day lay-over gave Brady concern about their success in trade with the Indians.

"Well, <u>well</u> Brady, we're <u>there</u>! Look at all them Injuns! Must be a couple hunnert of 'em! All painted up like . . ."

"Quiet Joe! Give the boss a hand tying up the boat. Where's Lisa? This must be the Mandan country. All the Redskins will be wantin' to trade. Men, women, don't seem to make no difference, they <u>all</u> like silver and brass doodads pinned all over 'em! No wonder there's big money to be made in this business."

"You're right Brady. Look at that big Indian standin' over there by hisself. He's got so much silver hangin' on him it's a wonder he can still walk. 'Peers to me, cousin, we might be a little too late to do any business here."

"No, I don't think so, but soon as we get ashore we better set up shop. We got goods that the squaws will like. They'll be real eager to trade. You'll see!"

"If we ain't careful Brady, old man Lisa might get mad at us for cuttin' in on his profits. What do you think?"

"You <u>blockhead</u>! We told the Captain that we planned to do some tradin' too. Don't you listen to anybody? He just laughed out loud, and some of them others that was standin' around did too. I guess he don't see much competition from the likes of us two, haw, haw! Well so be it then. I reckon 'Captain' Lisa, that's what they're calling him, even though he ain't no <u>real</u> captain, will buy any furs we get. Hope so. That way we won't have to pack anything back home but bags of silver money! Right, Joe?"

"Right Brady! Right as rain. Let's get ashore. Now what?"

Two burly buckskin-clad trappers, one of them their "boat boss", stood shoulder to shoulder at the gangplank, holding everyone back. Manuel Lisa was nowhere in sight. Evidently he had given orders that no one be allowed ashore until he had started the trading ritual.

"<u>Wowee</u>! Joe hissed. "There comes the Captain out of the woods yonder. Would you just look at him! He's wearin' a long coat that's as red as the old rooster. And them <u>boots</u>! Some poor slob musta spent a hour shinin' 'em up, don't you think?"

"Hush up Joe! Let's see what goes on. Look there! That big brave we saw, the one had all them doodads on him, is standin' right there waitin' for the Captain. More and more Injuns are crowding around too. It's quite a show, ain't it?"

Maklin-toa, one of the three main chiefs of the Mandan village, stood ramrod straight, arms folded and head thrown back. With a simple gesture he indicated that the crowd should approach and sit. The cleared area on the Missouri's western bank was soon filled, as nearly two thousand men, women, and children crowded near. Lisa strode forward, right hand up, palm forward. Four other white men, Lisa's business partners, all splendidly dressed, followed directly behind their leader.

"Hey Brady, look there kinda hid back of that guy with the top hat. Ain't that Tom Bluefoot?"

"It sure as shootin' is, Joe. And look who's skulking along behind them others. It's that Injun who threatened to cut Bluefoot's throat back in St. Louis. Listen cousin, we got to get over there! The Captain ain't paying no attention. Our friend's in trouble fer shore!"

"But them two by the gangplank won't let us past."

"Oh no? Come on Joe. Just be ready!"

The cousins moseyed closer, as if to see better. The two guards, fascinated by the activity ashore, were not paying close attention. Brady took two long steps, pushed one man into the river, then punched the other one in the stomach. Brady and Joe slammed the doubled-up guard aside, clattered down the ramp and raced up the bank toward Tom Bluefoot.

"Watch out Tom!" Joe yelled. "Behind you! He's got a knife!"

Manuel Lisa sprang to his feet, a look of rage darkening his handsome face. Such conduct was unheard of at the beginning of these delicate negotiations. "You there! Sammy George!" he shouted. "Put that knife away and sit down over there. Tom Bluefoot, come here next to me. I'll need you to translate as soon as the parlay begins."

Not to be dissuaded, the would-be interpreter, Sammy George, shouted out. "Him, no! No terperter. Me do! Me do! It me Sammy George do. Him, no!"

"You two men," Luis said out of the corner of his mouth, "shut him up." He indicated that Brady and Joe should take care of the furious interpreter. They had no trouble, as the Indian did not resist. The look of pure hatred on his face, however, indicated plainly enough that he was not intimidated, but had only acquiesced in deference to the delicate proceedings and the obvious rage of the expedition leader.

Captain Lisa turned calmly toward the chiefs before him. He then motioned to one of his followers and a small leather chest was put forward. He set it down and made motions that one of the Mandan chiefs should open it. Chief Tanego looked surprised.

Tom Bluefoot who was now sitting behind the others, inched forward and nudged Lisa's shoulder. Ignoring the Captain's look of extreme irritation, he said in a sort of sing-song monotone, "Not yet! You must smoke before any gifts are exchanged."

"You are right of course! After all my dealings with the red men I should have remembered this important detail. Pass the word that a pipe be brought up."

"No," Tom whispered, "the chiefs will produce the pipe at the proper time. There is more ceremony that must take place. For them it is . . ."

His words were suddenly interrupted by a furious shout from the forgotten interpreter, Sammy George. "Now you die <u>one-arm</u>!" he snarled, stiletto thrust low and forward.

Joe jumped in to help Tom, but he was grabbed and held back. A sort of low, growling sound began to grow among the seated citizens of the Mandan village. They had sensed an escalating conflict between two strangers in their midst. When a few rose hesitantly to their feet, more and more quickly followed. "Chi-wego! Chi-wego!" they began to chant in unison. They loved to watch a fight, especially one which might result in a combatant's death!

Captain Lisa rose uncertainly, glancing at the main chief. The Indian leader and his associates also stood and quickly quieted the crowd. With a word or two in their language they had Sammy and Tom dragged forward, arms pinned behind them, and forced to face each other.

The chiefs, seemingly delighted at this turn of events, ordered the onlookers back until their closely packed bodies created a human circle around the two men, perhaps twenty paces in diameter. Obviously they were expected to fight.

Sammy George, still brandishing his wicked little blade, glowered in rage. Toom-She-chi-Kwa looked terrified. He was not only unarmed, but also a man with the use of but one arm.

The Indian leaders had not yet given the order to release the two men and let the fight begin. Well they knew the value of anticipation! Each one made the customary short speech while the onlookers shifted and turned, anxious to see some blood!

Tom was sick with fear. "Hey Tom, it's us, Joe and me. Can we do anything to stop the fight? He'll gut you sure! Here! I'll toss you my knife. Don't let him get close or he'll be sure to . . ."

Brady's knife was slapped away and he and Joe were shoved roughly back from Tom and Sammy George. The circle kept closing in until finally a chief made a stern order that the fighters be given room. Another head man attempted to speak with Lisa, but with both interpreters still in the circle and ready to kill each other , Captain Lisa shrugged his shoulders. The Mandan leader took this as approval and barked an order.

Sammy George's upper lip stretched in a cruel sneer. This would be his chance to perform for the crowd. "Now one-arm. No man you! Now you belly open come. Sammy George, me stick! Stick! Ha! Me do!"

Lisa was sick at the prospect of losing such a valuable man as Tom Bluefoot, but there was nothing he could do. Leadership was an extremely tricky business, and he must walk a thin line when in the Indians' homeland. He must remain neutral.

Tom's eyes rolled in terror. He knew he was going to die very soon. Suddenly within his tortured brain the voice of his favorite, long dead uncle, Black Pipe, came clearly. "When death is near stand tall!"

Bluefoot stopped trying to sink into the ring of bystanders, squared his shoulders, and manged a look of calm. Sammy George advanced slowly, taking his time. He was playing to the crowd and enjoying every minute. "Now 'one-arm', now you me us we I Sammy George now I . . ."

"Cheswiga!" Cattail's scream shocked the onlookers as she smashed her way through the crowd, directly between the combatants. Confused, Sammy backed up a step but kept his knife extended.

"You go! You go now! Me," he snarled. "Now me . . ."

"Enough!" Manuel Lisa shouted, throwing caution to the winds. He leaped directly into the circle, swung Cattail behind him, and confronted the would-be interpreter. His face mottled with rage he encircled the girl with his left arm and with his right sent Sammy stumbling backward.

"Get out!" he roared. "Leave this village by sundown or be shot by my men. Only a coward attacks an unarmed man, especially one with only one useful arm. Your services are no longer needed. This man," he nodded at Tom, "is my only interpreter from now on. Remember, Sammy George, if you are seen in this camp or any other, I have given orders that you be shot. Now go!"

By now Sammy George had managed to regain something of his former bravado. He turned his back on the Captain, Tom, and the trembling Cattail. The crowd parted to let him pass, but as he stamped out he took a moment to lock eyes with Tom Bluefoot. His hatred was so intense it could almost be felt. It was obvious that he was not through dealing with this small handicapped man, regardless of what Manuel Lisa said. Tom was not aware of this development, as the whole scenario had paled with the approach of his grown-up daughter.

The two came together, tears of joy mingling on their cheeks. The crowd began to melt away, uninterested in such a boring display.

"So, my little Forest Flower, you intervene again, eh? Is running about and saving your step-father and now your real father all you do? Not only are you most lovely, but also courageous as well! My, my, what a prize the forest has handed us!" Lisa said.

The Mandan chief motioned impatiently for Captain Lisa to rejoin him and the others so the trading could be resumed. Lisa spoke briefly with the visibly shaken Tom Bluefoot, requesting that he still stay close to interpret. Tom however had his mind on other things! His daughter, Cattail, whom the Captain was calling "Forest Flower", would not leave his side, but Menseeta, her mother, hid her face in shame.

"What shall I do, husband?" she whispered to the angry and thoroughly confused Phillipe.

The Frenchman pulled loose from Menseeta's arm and charged toward Cattail and Tom. "These be my wife, my daughter!" he exploded, yanking the girl from her true father. "I, Phillipe," he shouted, "am Pa-Pa' to zis girl. Him," he jabbed Tom with a finger, "he abandon zem! Phillipe claim zis woman and her daughter as my own. Who fed them? Who teach ze French to both? Me, Phillipe!"

"You are wrong, Frenchman! Menseeta is my legal wife and this girl is my daughter. Both were with me at the Battle of Fallen Timbers where I was shot and my oldest daughter was killed."*

*Read Harnishfeger's first novel in the Tom Bluefoot trilogy: Tom Bluefoot, Wyandot Scout, General "Mad Anthony" Wayne, and the Battle of Fallen Timbers," available from Trafford Publishing Company.

"Hold! Hold! What is all this? Stand apart, you two." Lisa's words defused the situation instantly. Even the head chief of the Mandans stood up and approached the growing crowd. Lisa placed a protective arm around the beautiful young Forest Flower. Both Tom and Phillipe began a rapid defense of their position in the situation. Lisa, uninterested in trying to follow either one, gave another command. "This is all that I will hear at this time. Such harangue dishonors the great Mandan chiefs and their associates. There is important work to be done here for the benefit of both red men and white. Such a display is rude. Rude!"

"But Monseur," Phillipe began angrily, "this man has no right to . . ."

"I said enough!" Captain Lisa growled. "This is what is to be done. Forest Flower, you and your mother go to my tent and remain there until the trading is finished. You two men, separate yourselves from each other in this village. Have no other words between you. If you do, both will be driven out. I will call for you when I am through here. Is that clear?"

Both men nodded, but neither was happy and neither was satisfied.

All the principal participants were finally re-seated, but it was obvious that the Mandan chief was angry about the delay. The trading would not go well on this day in late October, 1807. Lisa would have to work without an interpreter.

Tom headed away from the crowd, his senses in a whirl. He had just seen his wife for the first time in almost seven years, and his beloved daughter, now nearly a grown woman. But what caused the awful throbbing ache in his heart was the picture of Menseeta, whether married or not, traveling with this short, stocky Frenchman and holding what was obviously their baby. Added to his misery was his fear of what Manuel Lisa might decide was to be done regarding which "husband" would be declared the right one. He sat down at the base of a tree, his head in his hands.

"You got a hurt arm."

Tom wiped a tear from his cheek and looked up in surprise. A boy of perhaps ten winters stood there holding a length of rawhide. "Thou speaketh English," Tom said stupidly.

"You seen my dog?"

"No. No . . . I haven't . . . seen, but . . ."

"He runned off. If you be the one as finds him he's still mine! You got that do ya?"

Toom-she-chi- Kwa rose unsteadily and gave a searching look at the lad. "Why . . . why . . . are you a <u>white</u> child?"

"What be 'white'?"

"Thou speakest like the Shemanese. Where did you learn that? Are you a captive?"

"I ain't captured. Well no more I ain't. You want to talk to my ma?"

"Your mother is here <u>too</u>?" Tom gasped. "Yes! Take me to her right away! Don't wait for . . ."

"But my doggie . . ."

"I'll help you find your dog later. Trust me. Now please show me where you mother is."

"<u>Tom</u>! Tom Foot!" The call echoed along the slowly moving Missouri.

There could be no doubt who was shouting. "That you, Joe? I'll be there in a minute. Hang on."

"You gotta come <u>now</u> Tom!" Joe bellowed, elbowing his way through the willows. "Captain Lisa sent mc to bring you right back to his tent. He wants to settle that business as to you and the Frenchie. He don't cotton to waitin' neither."

"I'm coming Joe," he yelled. Turning, he grabbed the boy's arm and said, "You come right back here in about an hour or so and wait for me. I'll give you a gift if you do. Now don't forget will you?"

"Come on Tom! We gotta get goin'!"

When they entered Lisa's tent they could see that the Captain was not in a happy mood! First the interruptions during the trading, and now this ridiculous situation regarding a French man, and Indian man, two Indian women, and a baby! How was he to adjudicate this mess?

"You sit over there, and Tom Bluefoot on the other side. Floret Fleur, take this chair on my right, your mother on my left."

"Monseur Lisa," Phillipe began, "I wish to tell you . . ."

"Be quiet! I will tell you when to speak. Each will be given an opportunity to tell his or her side of the story. Let me assure you my friends, when all the talking is done I will make my judgment. The decision will be final and there will be no appeal.

Is that clear?" No one said a word so he continued. "As a gentleman and with proper respect I ask the daughter, whom I call Floret Fleur, to be the first to speak." His obsession with the young Wyandot maiden was not unnoticed by anyone present. Tears running down her cheeks, the girl could say nothing. Torn by conflicting emotions, she only shook her head and continued crying.

Manuel Lisa, always the gentleman, tried hard to hide his impatience. He turned to the mother, touched her arm and smiled charmingly. "Now you, woman. What can you tell me about this situation? Were it up to you, how would you solve the dilemma?"

Although Menseeta had often spoken English during her years with Toom-She-chi-Kwa, much had been forgotten. Some of Captain Lisa's words were unknown to her as well, but she spoke up at last.

"What you ask, Monseur, is not p;possible for me." She turned a loving eye upon her husband, Tom, who was sitting dejectedly against the tent's main support pole. "Toom-She-chi-Kwa cared for me when I was a widow with a little boy. We then had two girls of our own. The oldest was shot to death at the Fallen Timbers fight. The other sits at your side."

"And what of the boy?" Lisa asked politely.

"His name is 'Red Gopher ' in the English tongue. At the proper time he moved in with my brother, his uncle, to learn the ways of the warrior. You remember him, do you not?" she asked Tom. He nodded almost imperceptibly but head hanging, did not meet her eyes. "Where my son is now or even if he lives I do not know. Flat Lance did well with him but that man, my brother, he died of the spotted sickness."

"A sad story madame, but unfortunately one not unusual in these times. So . . ." he paused for a moment, "since this man is your true husband, and the father of this lovely 'Flower of the Forest', I take it you choose to return as wife to Tom Bluefoot. Not so?"

"Wait! Wait!", Phillipe cried, jumping up. "What is all zis? No one ask Phillipe to speak! Menseeta not tell ze story of me, Pnhillipe. So I tell. After years as a voyageur I decide to do ze trading to get rich. Then . . ."

"Please sit back down Monseur Phillipe. I wish to hear what this woman has to say about you, just as she did about my interpreter, who is called Tom Bluefoot."

"It is well. My heart is torn inside of me," Menseeta moaned miserably. "How can I choose between two fine men who have . . ."

"This is craziness!" Phillipe shouted. "Tell ze Captain how I, Phillipe, take you in when you had nossing. <u>Nossing!</u>"

Lisa rose angrily and was about to admonish the Frenchman when Menseeta raised a hand. "It is well Captain and Leeza. It is well. Cattail and me and new baby, we owe much to that man. He be right when he say we had nothing. Not true, Cattail?"

"It is true my mother. I remember that hungry it was then. Very hungry then yes! Phillipe want me call him Pa-Pa' now. I do it because . . ."

The proceedings were suddenly interrupted by the entrance of the Mandan Indian woman who had served them. She hurried up to the table, leaned close to Manuel Lisa, and spoke softly to him.

"The Mandan chief demands to know why the trading has not progressed. My entire operation is in jeopardy should we not get the furs these Mandans have brought to trade. The issue of which man is to accept the role of husband must be settled immediately. Madame Menseeta you must decide. Speak now!"

Menseeta, uncharacteristically rose and stood next to Tom who was still sitting by the tent pole. She placed a loving hand on his cheek, but before she could speak Phillipe was again on his feet. A look of outrage twisted his swarthy features.

Lisa stopped him with a raised hand and a steely glance. "Make your choice, little mother," he demanded, not unkindly. "We are far from any sort of law here in this wilderness, and therefore as leader of this operation I seek the best solution to an admittedly complicated problem. As I, Manuel Lisa, see it, the one who has most at stake is this woman. Please Madame, you <u>must</u> choose."

Menseeta's hand slid to Tom's shoulder. He looked up hopefully, but was completely shattered by her first words. "As it has been since Manitou made the earth, we, us . . . we womens need to make sure our ones . . . we love are . . . how you say it, cared for. Toomie here a good man he good one man. He kind. He smart! Very smart he. But he get shot now only one arm good one. I Menseeta have new baby. Phillipe gone get rich one day. Baby need Menseeta. Philippe he is Papa of new baby. Philippe work hard he get rich one day. He march, march, <u>march</u>! We go to Philippe. He care for us, we get rich too!"

Tom rose, head hanging and quietly left the tent.

"It is settled then!" Lisa pronounced as he practically ran from the tent.


\*          \*          \*


Simon, "The Dancer" handed his third child back to her mother. "Call the Main Ones to meet at Buffalo Puller's lodge," he said as Polly, his first wife prepared to leave with the baby. "Our village must prepare for a trip far to the north."

"To the <u>north</u>?" Polly asked in alarm. "But why Dancer King? Why must we leave here? And why <u>now</u>? Soon the trails will be choked with snow. Most of the men will be leaving for the fall hunt, since the buffalo will be moving toward the far valleys. There will be no . . ."

"That is all I will hear from you. All will be made clear at the meeting of the Main Ones. Find your sister. Arrange for young Stone Saver to put the girl babies to bed. Bring my son, Ripe Pumpkin, and Beth, wife number two, with you to the meeting."

"The boy is not yet old enough to attend such a meeting, my husband. He will fall asleep and shame you before the Elders."

Simon chuckled fondly. "You are probably right, wife number one. That boy seems to be good at only two things; eating and sleeping. Bring him anyway. I want him to see how his father, Dancer King, is honored in a council of the Main Ones."

"Why are you meeting in the night this time, Simon? The Main Ones will not be happy about that."

The black former slave scowled at his wife. "I have ordered you not to use that name! You know that it angers me. I wish to forget my days in bondage. That was the name my mother gave me, but now I am 'Dancer'. Dancer <u>King</u>!"

"Oh, I am <u>so</u> sorry, Mr. Dancer King!" she said, grinning openly. Unlike her sister Beth, Simon's other wife, she was not intimidated by the man's posturing. After all they had been with him for over six years since they'd left the Kickapoos. Ordered to go west of the Mississippi to find a suitable new home territory for a small Sept of the Kickapoo Nation, it seemed that Dancer King had forgotten their mission. His only goal had been to get as far from re-capture by his former master as possible. For that reason he had led the band beyond the Father of Waters all the way to the banks of the Missouri.

"Mr. Dancer King," she said, bowing slightly again in mock derision, "and what of the Otoe? Will they not wonder about the secrecy of this meeting?"

"Ah, you little mink, were you not such a pretty little thing I would use a switch on you!" His laugh proved his fondness for the outspoken wife number one. "As I have already told you, everything will be made clear this night. However, you may be right about our neighbors, the Otoe."*

"They have been good to us Simon . . . I mean Dancer. Remember two winters ago when all of us were nearly starving? They shared what little they had and even brought firewood to our lodge." She stood and prepared to leave, but kept a bold eye on her husband's face.

Dancer didn't answer for a moment, but then said, "This much I will tell you now. The rest you will learn tonight. While it is true that the Otoe have not objected to our camp being so near to their village, they seemed to be less friendly at their last Council gathering. I, as Dancer King, was asked to attend, but they did not permit our Main Ones. This seemed a little strange, but I decided not to say much about it."

"Well you certainly didn't say anything to <u>me</u>! Nor to my sister either.

*The Otoe [also spelled Oto] was a Native American tribe whose territory lay between the Omaha on the north and the Kansa to the south, in what would one day be parts of Kansas, Oklahoma and Nebraska.

Lewis and Clark made contact with the Otoe nation in July, 1804 as they proceeded west on their historic "Corps of Discovery" expedition.

You should learn to trust your wives more than you do," she chided.

With the moon rising slowly over the treetops, Dancer and his wives joined the Main Ones in Buffalo Puller's more spacious lodge. The substantial pole and bark dwelling was so heated by the central fire that all were sweating, even before the always extensive speeches began.

Six-year-old Ripe Pumpkin, to his mother's surprise, was wide awake. His dark eyes missed nothing of the ceremonially-dressed Main Ones.

Beth quickly joined the several other Indian women seated along one wall of the lodge.

Ripe Pumpkin pulled free from his mother's hand and marched up to his father. Ignoring the disapproving scowls of the four Elders, he plopped himself down directly in front of Dancer King.

"Dancer King," one said, "is it not bad enough that we must tolerate the presence of these women? Now your son, no more than six or seven winters old, has joined us also. We wish to show no disrespect, but . . ."

"Of course! You need an explanation of these unusual proceedings. My son," he placed one hand on the lad's shoulder, "is one of the main reasons I have asked you to leave your sleeping robes for this meeting." Ripe Pumpkin puffed out his small chest and glanced around importantly.

An Elder spoke up. "I would speak first as is my right as "Council Talker" of our Sept."

"That is as it should be, but tonight it would not be wise. Our time may be cut short," Dancer continued hurriedly. "I do not wish for the Otoe to know what we decide here."

"This no threat," Council Talker interrupted, angry that he would not be able to make the speech he had prepared when so hastily summoned to the night meeting. "After all, why should we keep secrets from our friends? They have been good to . . ."

"It is true," Dancer broke in, "but only I was permitted to attend their last Council meeting. As you know they did not invite anyone else from our camp. Had you been there you would have been certain to notice the anger in their eyes, if not in their voices."

"But why?" one of the others asked. "We have been careful to stay away from their villages, their gardens, even their hunting and fishing sites."

"That is also true, Hunter. But now," Simon lowered his voice and glanced around nervously, "the red-speckled sickness* has come upon three of their women, as it once did in past years. They are afraid and they are <u>angry</u>!"

"What is that to us?" Council Talker growled.

"As you all know I was once a slave to a white family. When someone was angry or afraid they always looked for someone else to blame. We slaves were usually the ones chosen. In that same meeting, Looks Back, one of their main chiefs, pointed out that no one in our camp has yet been visited by the red dots on our faces and chests. If that weren't bad enough, Rattler, a bad man who wants to be their medicine man and seer, said that he had been having a dream which told him that we are trying to curse them with the little red dots sickness. He said that we wished to see them all dead so we could get their goods and their horses!"

"Why didn't you tell us this before?" Council Talker shouted.

"I thought nothing would come of it, but now the little red spots have fallen on two more Otoe women and one child. Perhaps your king has been wrong in not calling you Elders together sooner. Who can say? What is important now is that we must leave this place and follow the river north."

"Leave? Leave our fine lodges? Our gardens?" one of the sisters cried.

"Why to the north?" an Elder demanded. "The cold moons are coming. And coming <u>soon</u>! This does not seem to be a good plan to me." He glanced around the lodge. Several were nodding in agreement.

"We shall reach out to the Arikara, as those people are natural enemies of the Otoe. We should be safe there," Dancer said.

"Safe? Safe from the Otoe? They are not our enemies. What are you saying?" Council Talker was confused and angry.

"Because my good friend, if the Otoe chiefs are convinced by this evil one trying to become their medicine man that their sickness is our fault we will be <u>driven</u> out. There will be no time to pack our goods, prepare proper clothing, and make other preparations. Then as soon as we are gone they will take everything we have worked for. That is why."

"Has Chief Looks Back told you this?" an Elder demanded rudely.

*Native Americans, having no built-up immunity, were especially susceptible to such illnesses as measles, influenza, and cholera. Land-hungry pioneers often exploited this weakness in horrible ways. "Smallpox blankets" which had been in contact with infected white persons were sometimes given to the Indians. Entire villages were often nearly wiped out by the rapidly spreading infection.*

"No, he did not <u>tell</u> me. Not in words. But as my wives can tell you, I am often able to see into the hearts of men. How this happens I cannot say, and sometimes the ability does not come to me, but this time it did."

First wife Polly made a soft sound in her throat. When no one paid any attention she did it again, louder this time.

"Well what is it? Do you have something to say, woman?" an Elder demanded irritably.

"Many pardons! Many pardons!" she murmured, "but when Dancer King hears the words in his head they are <u>never</u> <u>wrong</u>!"

"Listen! Be <u>quiet</u> everyone!" second wife Beth suddenly hissed, pulling the door curtain aside. "Horses! Coming fast!" They all heard it then.

No one left Buffalo Puller's lodge, nor did they acknowledge their visitors, who could be heard securing their horses.

"Hello this lodge," a commanding voice called.

Dancer nodded to the Council Talker who stated firmly, "welcome to this house. You may enter."

Otoe chief Looks Back yanked the door curtain open and stalked inside. That he was angry there could be no doubt. Four other Otoes followed, not saying a word.

Dancer King tried to mollify the delegation. "Polly, prepare a pipe for our guests. We will smoke, and then . . ."

"There will be no need!" the chief interrupted. "We demand to know the reason for this secret gathering in the night."

"But chief Looks Back, this is but a friendly time of . . ."

"Be quiet, Dancer! You are no king, especially here in the territory of the Otoes. I have questions which you will answer."

For the first time, Council Talker spoke up, surprising them all with his courage. "You are in Buffalo Puller's lodge. Have you forgotten common courtesy and the correct procedure for the arrival of unexpected and uninvited guests?"

"Common courtesy you say?" one of the visitors snorted. "Where is the 'courtesy' in holding a secret and unannounced council meeting in the night hours?"

Dancer spoke, trying to hold his anger. "We know that you Otoes allow us to live close to your main village. We appreciate that. We also acknowledge that your people have often shared food with us when we had none. However," and here Dancer locked eyes with chief Looks Back for a moment, " it is also true that your braves have come demanding our corn, our beans, and even our tanned skins. We are <u>not</u> subject to you. We have made no such agreements. Furthermore . . ."

"Enough!" the chief thundered. "He Sees, we will hear from you now. Step forward."

He Sees, the aged and true Otoe Medicine Man, had been almost unnoticed in the hot and crowded lodge. A small man, he wore a beautifully beaded vest and silver arm bands. Five earrings dangled from each ear. What was most noticeable about him however was the shining silver "peace medal" resting proudly against his chest.

"Tell them, seer. Tell them of the vision," the chief said, shoving Council Talker and one of the women aside to make room for the seer.

He Sees held a small silver bell over his left shoulder and rang it softly twice. "Big Man come to me on three nights. That One showed this miserable Otoe that you, black man, that you , who claim to be a king, are planning to run away to our enemies, the Arikara. These subjects of their 'king'," he mocked, "will steal our horses to hurry them on their journey. Big Man has told all of this to the Seer. Also, the red spots sickness is from <u>you</u>! I have spoken."

It was now that that Simon [Dancer King] made use of his former years in slavery. Without a flicker of emotion showing on his face he hid his astonishment at the accuracy of the seer's vision. Pulling his son to his side, he answered.

"Your Medicine Man, as we have all heard, is a man touched by the gods. In only one thing is his vision not the truth. We had no intention of stealing your horses or anything else of yours. Still we humbly beg your pardon for our misguided plans. Thank you for setting us straight on such foolishness. We will be good neighbors and good servants to chief Looks Back and to all the Otoe."

Without another word the delegation left the lodge, mounted up, and rode off in the moonlight.

"You fool," Council Talker snarled. "Why did you let them speak to us in that way? Did you really plan to steal their horses?"

"Not at all! That would be stupid. Their youngest child could follow our tracks. We would be dragged back and made to be their slaves! I have come all these many months' journey to escape slavery. I have no intention of ever bearing that affliction again!"

"But . . .but . . ." Polly said, "you agreed with them! Never have I been ashamed of my husband before, but now . . ." All the others began voicing their agreement.

"Be quiet wife, all of you, listen to your king. They believe their seer. They also believe that what the white people call 'measles' is from us. They will not rest until we are driven out. Then they will take everything we have worked for in this place."

"Maybe we could fight them or defend ourselves in some way," an Elder suggested. Several groaned at the impossibility of such a thought.

Dancer did not dignify that suggestion with an answer. "Here is what we must do," Simon told them. "We will act as if ashamed. We will pretend that we have been found out, and that we are sorry about it. Then in five days' time in the hour before dawn we will leave."

"But they will know it. There is no way we can get away safely," Beth said, taking the now sleeping Ripe Pumpkin in her arms.

"You forget, wife two," the Dancer King smiled, "that your husband is a seer also. I too have had visions. They tell me that in three days the Otoe will move out on the plains to hunt buffalo. When they return we ill be gone. Gone far to the north!"

"Not all the Otoe will go on the hunt," Council Talker pointed out.

"Of course not. But those who do not go will be only old ones, nursing mothers, and small children. I also know of some tricks that will make it hard for them to follow."

"And where did you learn such 'tricks'?" an Elder asked skeptically.

"From my friend, Tom Bluefoot, or Toom-She-chi-Kwa in your language. We made a long escape from the whites who pursued us. I was running from my slave master. Tom had been wrongly accused of murder. Those from the white mans' laws were after him."**

"It will take a long time for you to teach all of this to us," Council Talker complained. Several heads were nodding in agreement.

Polly took the sleeping boy from her sister and boldly proclaimed, "My husband, Dancer King, is not only wise in the ways of men, but a true <u>seer</u> as well! As it has been since we Kickapoos were given the duty of finding new lands for our Sept, so it will be at this time. He will lead us, we will follow!"

Somewhat mollified, they continued discussing their plight and possible solutions until dawn was near.

** *Read Lloyd Harnishfeger's book, "Tom Bluefoot, Chief Tecumseh, and the War of 1812." available from Trafford Publishing Co.*

\*          \*          \*

"Where you been, mister? I found my doggie myself, so I don't need no help no more. I was settin' right there to wait for you to come, but ants got to bitin' me so I set over here by this . . ."

"What are you talking about?" Tom asked miserably. "Why are you still here waiting for me?" he asked, his mind still whirling from the shock of losing his wife and only remaining daughter.

"Why 'cause you said!" the lad replied. "You told me you wanted to meet my Ma, and I was to wait right here till you come. You said you'd help me find my doggie then too. Well I got him my own self, so . . ."

"Yes, yes, I remember. Your mother. Yes." He was mumbling almost incoherently. The boy eyed him suspiciously.

"Well you wanta go see Ma or not, do ya?"

"Well . . . well . . . I think . . . is it far?"

"What's wrong with you, Injun? You act like yo ain't got no sense! No it ain't far. Maybe a half an hour or so. Let's get goin'. Ma will be wonderin' about me. Come on doggie. You hongry? I am too! We're goin' to our camp." He set off at a fast walk, not caring if Tom followed or not.

The camp was farther than the boy had indicated, as it took Tom almost an hour to find it. Of course the boy was younger, and may have trotted part of the time.

The camp was like many others at that time and in that part of what would some day be called Oklahoma. The men and women appeared somewhat darker than those of the forests and woodlands. The sun and wind had done its work on them.

"Hello the camp!" Tom yelled while still a bowshot away. "Hello!" he repeated. A man approached, looking none too friendly.

"I am Fire Grass," he said in sign language. "Who you?"

Tom Bluefoot, still not very proficient in sign language, did his best but the brave finally shook his head in disgust. He was about to order Tom to leave when a shout startled them both.

"Tom! Hey Tom! I'm glad you finally got here." The lad spoke rapidly to the Cheyenne, Fire Grass, who relaxed and walked away. "I told Fire Grass who you was but he didn't say nothing back. You still want to see my Ma?"

"Yes I do," Tom asserted. "Is that your tepee over by that thicket?"

"No. We're way over yonder along the crick. Come on, I'll show you."

The woman was on her knees, fleshing out what appeared to be a staked-down buffalo hide. Hair side down, the skin looked enormous. Although dressed in the usual knee-length buckskin dress and tunic, the boy's mother was obviously Caucasian. She looked up in irritation at her son and the visitor. She rattled off a few words in the Cheyenne language and bent back to her work.

"Talk English, Ma. This here Injun can talk it better than me even."
The woman leaned back on her heels, wiped her brow on a sleeve, and studied Tom Bluefoot. "You speak English? Who are you and what are you doing here in our camp?"

"I am an interpreter for Manuel Lisa and his fur company. They are trading with the Mandans a short distance . . ."

"But why are you here? Our chief is Twa-tu-na. His name means something like 'he found it' in English. We had a few hides and three ponies to trade. That is done. We will leave for the south as soon as Twa-tu-na orders it. How did you learn to speak in Shemanese . . . I mean white man's talk?"

"Back in Pennsylvania I was bought from my drunken father by a Quaker man. He taught me."

"I see. Percy told me a little about you. I suppose Mr. Lisa and the fur company will also be leaving soon. What will you do then?"

"I think he wants me to accompany his organization, even though I know nothing about the languages of the tribes he plans to visit. Also, as you can see I'm only learning to do sign language."

"How did you ever get clear out here? I don't know where Pennsylvania is, but it must be a far piece from here."

"It's a long story," Tom sighed. "If Lisa doesn't leave for a few more days maybe I can visit you and the boy again."

"I guess we'll see," she said.

The boy spoke up then. "He told me he come out here to find a friend of hisn. Ain't that right Tom?"

"Yes. He's a black man, a slave who ran away from his master. He calls himself "Dancer" now. Have you heard of him at all?"

Both shook their heads. "I'm keeping you from your work," Bluefoot remarked. He glanced around in all directions then dropped to one knee and lowered his voice to a whisper. "Are you and the boy prisoners with these people? Maybe . . . maybe . . ." he peered around again, "maybe I can help you both escape. Manuel Lisa is getting ready to head north soon. He might be willing to hide you and Percy. Maybe I could . . ."

"Escape? What do you mean, Indian Tom? I am not a prisoner here, I could leave any time, and take Percy with me. I am happy here. Can you understand? Happy!"*

"I beg your pardon, Ma'am. I've overstepped myself."

"It's alright. You meant well." She leaned back over the buffalo hide and without pause continued speaking. "My husband, Asa, and I were trying to make a go of it back there on the plains. We were about out of food . Nothing seemed to grow there. Hardly any rain for most of the summer. Well, Percy was five or six years old, so it was getting time to think about some schooling for him. As for me, I was lonely and I was scared! We had no close neighbors and the army never came down that way. Asa kept thinking things would get better, but the worse it got, the meaner he got! He beat me a lot [she pointed to a scar above her eye] and he'd whale the tar out of little Percy too. I'd have left him but where would the boy and I go? We were miserable."

"I can see that you would have been," Tom said quietly. "So how did you wind up with these Indians?"

"The Cheyenne**came galloping in one early morning. They told me later that they were mainly after Tops and Tootsie."

"Oh my!" Tom gasped. "Were your girls just babies?"

Percy burst out laughing. "They was our mules"! He cackled. "Ma never had no more kids. I was the only one."

"I lost one, a tiny baby girl. It could have been because  when I was pretty far

*Surprising as it may seem, captured Anglo-Americans when found or ransomed, sometimes adamantly refused to be re-repatriated. If forced to do so they were usually miserably unhappy, and unable to adjust. Two of the most well-known examples are John Swearingen, adopted by the Shawnees and named "Blue Jacket", and Cynthia Ann Parker, the mother of Quanah Parker, the famous [or infamous] war leader of the Comanche Nation.

along, Asa had one of his mad fits. We were trying to put up some hay we had cut. Being in the family way, I was slow and awkward, but was doing my best to help. The hay was pitifully thin and not much of it. I was to do the raking up while Asa loaded the wagon. I guess I wasn't doing it fast enough. Asa started cussing me. He yanked the rake out of my hands and rammed the handle into my stomach. The baby was born dead that night. Percy you go down the crick a ways and fill the gourd with fresh water. You don't need to be hearing what I've been telling Mr. Tom right now."

"How sad for you! Percy didn't know about this then?"

"No. There was no need to tell him about that. He liked his Pa, and most of the time they got along . I hope this doesn't cause him to have terrible memories of his father."

"What happened to him?"

"Percy? He's fine. He'll be along with the water gourd soon."

*Some time around the sixteen hundreds the Cheyenne people migrated from their ancestral home near Lake Superior to the vast grasslands of the West. Subsequently their sedentary lifestyle of gardening, gathering, and small game hunting gave way to the pursuit of the American bison [buffalo].

Introduction of the horse to their people rapidly and dramatically changed their entire way of life. The annual fall hunt could bring down enough of the huge, seemingly numberless creatures to supply food, clothing, and nearly everything else needed for an entire winter, thus allowing time for other pursuits, such as raiding enemy camps, holding ceremonial gatherings, and building cultural alliances.

As their numbers increased and their horsemanship improved, they soon became a fierce and much-feared tribe, noted for their ruthless attacks, swift retreats, and courage.

No longer living in the earth-covered lodges of their past lives, the Cheyennes' adoption of the tipi [tepee] used by the Sioux and other dwellers of the plains, provided easy re-location when game became scarce or other reasons favored new environs.

The tribe eventually split to form the Northern and Southern bands.

"No, I meant your husband. What happened to him?"

Caroline continued to work, dragging the elk horn scraper steadily back and forth across the hide. "Like I said," she continued, "the Cheyenne raiding party came charging in just after sun-up. Asa was in the shed,hitching up the mules. As soon as he saw them coming he ran for the house to get his rifle. They rode him down and tomahawked him right there in our little yard."

"You saw all of this?" Tom asked sadly.

"I did.  I shoved little Percy under the table and grabbed the rifle off the pegs. But before I could bar the door Elk Hoof busted his way in. He grabbed the gun by the barrel, tore it out of my hands, and knocked me down with his fist. I jumped up, got hold of his necklace, and tried to scratch his eyes out. He knocked me down again. This time I couldn't get up. Percy jumped out from under the table and tried to kick him in the shins,"  she took the water gourd and set it down, "didn't you  honey?"

"I did Ma. I did for shore, but he just laughed."

"It's a wonder the Cheyenne didn't kill you both for fighting him like that!"

Caroline smiled as she worked. "Elk Horn told me later that fighting him was what saved my life. And Percy's too. He said he admired anyone who would fight for his own."

"Elk Horn treats me real good," Percy said proudly. "He made me a good bow, and showed me how to put feathers on my arrows." He paused for a moment then said, "I never call him Pa though."

"So . . . so . . . this Elk Horn is now your  . . . your man?"

"Yes. He is a good man too. He beat me a few times when we were first taken, but he explained later that it was expected because . . ."

"He never beat Ma real hard, Injun Tom," Percy spoke up loyally. "A time or two he walloped me too, but I had it comin', I did. Me and Yeller Feather, we don't get along too good. Elk Horn had him before he caught Ma and me. I don't know what happened to Yeller Feather's ma."

"She died of some sort of sickness," Caroline supplied. Tom said nothing, but a tear trickled down his cheek.

"I suppose I'd better be getting back to Manuel Lisa's camp. He may be looking for me. I don't want to go. I'm sure to run into my wife and daughter. Losing them is like a knife in my heart."

"Tom! Tom Bluefoot!" It was Joe again. "You better get back to camp, wherever you are. Come on!" He appeared at the edge of the clearing, glancing around at the scene before him. "The Captain's madder than a settin' hen with boils! He says that if you ain't back in a hour he'll kick you out! And maybe me and Brady too. I'm gettin' tired of chasin' you down. Who's the squaw? Wait a minute, is she a white woman? That her boy there? He shore enough ain't no full-blood Injun. Never mind. Just come on. If we cut through the woods we can maybe get back in time. I been huntin' you for almost a hour already!"

"Goodbye Caroline, Percy. Here's the gift I promised the boy."
He tossed over a small jack-knife. "There's more I could tell you, but as you can see . . ."

Joe grabbed Tom's good arm and practically dragged him into the forest.

*    *    *

"Look, my father! Horses! Look at that big white one. Why are they coming to our lodge?"

"Run and find your mother. Have her come here," Dancer ordered, shading his eyes against the morning sun. He watched as three riders dismounted and walked their horses boldly into what Dancer grandly referred to as his "courtyard".

Polly hurried up and took position behind her husband, keeping one hand on little Pumpkin.

"Welcome Otoes," Dancer cried. "Leave your horses. My woman will bring a pipe and we will smoke."

"We have no time for such foolishness. We have a message for all of you misplaced Kickapoos," one of the delegation replied. "I am Climber. We have come at the bidding of Chief Looks Back. You will call your Elders together so that all may hear what our chief says to you."

The three braves were little more than boys, but were obviously proud of being provided with fine horses and chosen as messengers to Dancer's people. They glanced around, curious about these strangers living in their territory.

"Again I say welcome to you three young braves. Sadly I cannot grant your request at this time. Two of our Elders are off hunting deer in the marshes east of us. As to the others, I have no idea where they are."

The delegation looked at each other uncertainly. "Send runners to find them and get them here," one of the boys, whose name was Climber, finally ordered.

"Once again I must apologize. The hunters have been gone for two days. They would be hard to locate. As for the others, who can say where they might be by now. Why not tie up your horses and come into my lodge. We have food and tobacco. Then after . . ."

"Pah!" their spokesman snorted. "I've told you before, we have no time for that. We will . . ."

"Let me suggest something," Dancer said, smiling. "I can see that Looks Back has certainly chosen three of his finest young braves for this mission. You will need to have a fitting answer when you make your report to him." Polly jabbed him with an elbow, a scowl marking her usually cheerful countenance. "Why not," Dancer continued, ignoring wife number one's obvious disgust, "tell your chief that you must return here in three days. By then I, Dancer King, will have had time to assemble our Elders. You three men can then inform all of us of Looks Back's orders."

Climber squared his shoulders, expanded his skinny chest, and replied, "Ah so! It is exactly what I was about to suggest. We go." They turned their horses and left, heading south toward the Otoe village.

"Sometimes . . . sometimes my husband . . ." Polly sputtered, "sometimes I think the moon has robbed you of your senses! Why did you allow those three mere boys to treat you so haughtily? If I were king I would have chased them away with a willow switch on their bottoms! Insolent pups! What kind of leader will they tell their people that you are? We will be made to be as nothing in their sight!"

"Exactly, good wife. The less they respect us the better. When we make our escape they will be completely unprepared."

"Perhaps. Perhaps. But it still is a thorn in my thumb to see such ones show you no respect. Now if I were . . ."

"Quiet! I have an errand for you. You must be quick."

"What is it now? More begging?"

"In a way, yes. Grab a few ears of corn and a pinch of tobacco. Run and catch up with those 'great warriors' who are walking their horses along the river. Tell them it's a gift for Chief Looks Back."

"A gift? They will laugh in my face."

"Good! Apologize for such a meager offering, but explain that it is almost all we have."

Polly, smiling at last, hurried away to comply. "He is smart, and he is clever," she thought. "Everything we do now must convince the Otoes that we are not leaving." She trotted off, following the three riders' tracks.

Before she could return, Dancer summoned the Elders [who, of course were not as far away as he had told the Otoe boys]. As soon as all had smoked and rested he began. "What of our preparations Council Speaker? Is food being made ready and hidden?"

The Main Elder was excited. "Well! It is going well! Corn, pemmican, jerky, all wrapped in skins and tied for the journey." The others nodded and told of their work and what their wives and children were doing to get ready. "There is a problem however," he concluded.

"What is it?"

"It's the women. They refuse to leave their Shemanese tools and utensils."

"My wife says the same thing," Moon Dog groaned. "I told her what you said, Dancer King, that it must look as if we had just left our lodges for berry-picking or seining for fish in the creek. If they find we are gone it should appear that we are coming back."

"Good for you Moon Dog. After all, what woman would leave on a journey without taking her knife and her cooking pot? However if we are to escape, almost everything must be left behind."

For the next two days the Kickapoos made ready for what would certainly be a perilous journey.

The following night another visitor arrived at Dancer's lodge. As was customary, the man and boy called out before they were at the lodge's door opening. "We have come. We seek entry to this lodge."

"Who is out there?" wife number two whispered. "It's almost sunset!"

Dancer rose from the backrest where he'd been sitting. Pumpkin jumped up too. "They are from the Otoe camp, father," the boy said, peeking out of the door flap. "A man of power and a boy of maybe ten summers."

"Yes, it is the Otoe Medicine Man, 'He Sees'. Do you remember him? I knew he was coming here. I saw him in my head. He has the boy with him to lead the pony and carry his equipment."

The wives were not surprised. In their travels they had often been able to witness Dancer's "second sight". It had helped them on many occasions.

Polly, however, looked closely at her son.

"You may enter, honored Seer," Dancer said in a commanding but polite voice.

The elderly, beautifully dressed spiritual leader of Looks Back's band stepped inside without a word. As before, his black eyes took deliberate notice of everything in sight. His gaze came to rest on Ripe Pumpkin, Dancer and Polly's six-year-old son. Taking two steps forward, he placed a gentle hand on the boy's head. The normally shy child made no move, but locked eyes with the visitor for a long moment. The Medicine Man then turned to the Dancer King and asked gravely, "Does he have 'the gift' as well?"

Stunned, there was a pause until Polly answered. "We believe that he does but it will take more time until we can be sure."

He Sees nodded in agreement. "This one will become known throughout our world, especially to those who make the laws of the Shemanese people. Those who live in a place of many, many white people, and," he looked directly at Dancer, "many black people as well. Now child, we will talk together. Tell me about how it is with you when you 'see things in your head'. Can you tell what will happen in many coming days?"

"No, not many. Maybe this many days," He held up three chubby fingers.

"It is good! As you get older you will learn to look far into the future. A day will come when many will know your name, but it will not be Pumpkin then. It will be Victor."

The father, mother, and aunt were speechless. No one knew what to think, much less what to say. Finally Dancer King asked the Seer a question. "Why are you here, He Sees? What can we do for you?"

Nonplussed, the Medicine Man turned toward the door opening. He looked back, then motioned for Dancer to come outside. When Polly moved to follow them he held up a gentle hand to stop her. Without another word the two men left the lodge. Dancer followed as He Sees led the way to the edge of the clearing. The Otoe boy who had accompanied him started to follow but he stopped the lad with a quiet word.

"I ask again, why are you here? What is it that you want this night?"

"Do you believe that I have 'The Power'?"

"Of course! I saw that before when you came here with your chief."

"Good. If more proof is needed let me say that as I said then, I know of your plans to leave us, even though some of my people do not believe me."

"But . . . but . . . we are not . . . we're just . . ."

"Do not speak more to me, but only listen. I have told <u>no</u> <u>one</u> of what the latest visions have shown me. Nor will I do so now. I have come to help you and your people. Whether you believe me or not does not matter."

"Pardon an interruption," Dancer said. "I do believe that you can see into the hearts and minds of others. I also have no choice but to believe that you know of our plans. You have it in your power to do us great harm. I am thankful that you will not expose us. But why . . . I mean why are you . . .". Dancer could not find proper words to continue.

"Ah, so! You have reason to ask. I will answer your questions. It is true that Looks Back is planning to come upon you. He will kill some and make slaves of the others. In five days' time our tribe has been told to leave for the fall buffalo hunt. The chief has further ordered an attack on your small village the day before we leave. Your men, women, and boys who are not killed or wounded will be forced to follow us to the 'great grassy place'. They will be made to do the work of skinning and butchering the shaggy beasts that are taken."

"But we would . . ."

"Fight us?"

"Yes! Our men are strong, and there is no sickness among us."

"Do not be a fool. Bravery and courage are much admired by our people, but no one reveres one whose pride overrides what cannot succeed."

"I know that you are right in what you say," Dancer conceded, frowning in concern.

"As to your clan's good health, I am glad for you," He Sees continued. "You will certainly need it on the journey you will be undertaking. However the fact that you have no sickness here is the main reason the Otoes accuse you of witch-craft. What conjurer would bring disaster on his own people?"

"We hardly know what to say to show our gratitude," Dancer murmured.

He Sees continued speaking, the growing darkness making it almost impossible to see the prophet's expression.

"I am here for two reasons. First, you ill be surprised to learn that I also spent years in slavery. Captured by Arikara raiders when but a child, I was forced to watch the torture and murder of my mother. It was when she finally took her last breath that I felt 'the power' come onto me."

"That was a sad thing for a boy to go through. Believe me."

"Please!" He Sees said, "do not interrupt. There is much that I must tell you, and I dare not be gone from the Otoes much longer. The Arikara bound my legs every night for one year. It was cruel and unnecessary. How could a mere child escape from them anyway? I used that time to learn more about my special powers and how to use them. Forced to do 'woman's work' and beaten regularly, I made a secret vow. I would fight the evil of slavery whenever and wherever I found it. That is the first reason. I will not allow the Otoes to know that you will be going away from us."

"We humbly thank you for such a kindness. We are grateful!"

Again ignoring the interruption, He Sees continued. "Given wisdom beyond my years, I had never told the Arikara of my 'second sight'. When a vivid and compelling vision came upon me I divined that some Otoes raiders, seeking revenge, would be making an attack on the following morning. I chewed through my bonds and ran away to their war camp. They took me in. When I arrived at their camp they called me Bah-ra'-ta, 'New Boy'. That would not be a good name for me now would it?" he cackled with a toothless grin.

"All went well for me for many years until a proud young man named 'Rattler' appeared at our village. He claimed to be a Medicine Man, and convinced our chief that I was too old to be of use anymore. Sadly, many of the people I had helped or cured of sickness agreed with Rattler. A good name for him!"

"But He Sees, you were here with Chief Looks Back and agreed that we were the ones spreading the red dot sickness. I thought you agreed."

"Ah ha! Dancer King, you are well versed in trickery are you not? I had to agree with the evil Rattler. He was stirring up the people, especially the younger ones. My gift told me that my time with the Otoes was short. I am ready to let others lead, but at his insistence they would have banished me. Where would I go? What could I do? So now I am here. I intend to fulfill my vow by helping you on your way.

Whether you will succeed or not, Big Man has not seen fit to tell me. But now I will rest in peace when the owl calls my name."

"I cannot tell you how much this means to me and my people. Do not fear, I can well understand your position. In my former world, sometimes when a slave became too old to work, he or she would be what their owners called 'turned out'. With no place to go and no skills to offer, they usually did not live long after that happened."

The Seer's next words so shocked the Dancer that his mind was sent reeling.

"The second reason I kept your secret is that in your child, Ripe Pumpkin, I see an astonishing image of myself at his age. He <u>must</u> be saved! He will become, first of all a healer of great power. A healer not only of sickness and hurt, but a healer of relations as well. That boy when but a young man will be able to show our people the futility of constant strife and warfare! He will be asked to go far to the east to meet with chiefs of many tribes, and Shemanese of great power and influence. Again I say it! He <u>must</u> be saved, nourished, and allowed to develop his gift. See that he masters many tongues, both white and red. The lives of many will depend upon what he will say and do."

"Many pardons Grandfather," the Otoe boy called, using the universal title of respect, "but you told me that before the moon is seen over the treetops we must . . ."

"Yes! Yes! We go." Both started south as fast as the boy could lead the pony.

"<u>Wait</u>! Wait, please!" Dancer called. "You could come <u>with</u> <u>us</u>! We will protect you. Also . . ."

"That cannot be. I am too old to walk, and you must not leave the tracks of a horse. Also, I am truly needed by the Otoes. I must call the buffalo to ensure a successful hunt. Otherwise there will be crying during the hunger moon."

They were gone.

Dancer practically stumbled his way into the lodge, his black face appearing white in the firelight.

"What is it?" Beth cried. "You look about to faint. Are we undone? Do the Otoes know of our plans? What . . ."

"Summon Elder Talker!" Dancer said.

Polly, looking with concern at her stricken husband, spoke up. "But it grows late. Elder Talker has already met with you. He will be getting ready for sleep."

"Go to his lodge. If he sleeps, wake him. Get him here. <u>Now</u>!"

"I ask again," second wife Beth said, "are we to expect an attack?"

"No, wife of my two little girls. The news is good, but we must re-double our efforts. Pumky," he said to the boy, "come here and sit at my feet. Do not talk! Listen as carefully as you are able. Are you ready?"

"I am, my father, but please don't call me Pumky anymore. Either use my true name of The People, or just Pumpkin as it is in the Shemanese."

"I'll remember," Dancer grinned. "Now Pumpkin, sometimes you have been able to see the weather that will come. We must know what lies ahead."

"I will go outside," the boy said proudly.

He was gone for only a few minutes. Not a word was spoken while he was outside, nor for a moment when re re-entered the lodge. "Well," Polly asked, "what can you tell your father?"

"Snow comes. <u>Big</u> snow!"

Dancer was elated. "Can you tell us when the snow will come to us?"

Pumpkin frowned in concentration, then held his chubby left hand before them. Slowly, using the first finger of his right hand he touched each finger in turn. "At this finger day Snow Maker is here," he said calmly, touching his fourth finger. "Now, Aunt Beth, I should be given a piece of maple candy. A <u>large</u> piece!"

All laughed in delight.

"It is good!" Dancer exclaimed. "We will leave the night before the snow comes. With luck, or the help of Manitou, or perhaps the white man's God, Jehovah, our tracks will be covered with enough snow that no one will be able to follow. Give Pumky . . . I mean Pumpkin, <u>two</u> pieces of maple candy!"

At first light on the following day Dancer King called a council meeting of every adult. Men, women, and even the three boys of at least twelve winters were quickly assembled. With a piece of buckskin on the lodge's packed dirt floor he used a charred stick to show each one what he was to do, three mornings later.

"Keep a fire going in your lodges. Throw on a few green branches so there will be plenty of smoke rising from the roof vent. Have a stew pot simmering by the fire. Go out by twos as if you were gathering berries. At first make sure your tracks are plain, but a little later make you trail as confusing as possible. Proceed a ways then walk backward in your own moccasin prints. Jump sideways off the trail. Anything you can do to keep any followers busy will give us more time to keep going north."

Dancer continued giving both orders and suggestions. "Where did you learn all of this?" Council Speaker asked in surprise. "You have only been living like The People for a short time."

Dancer paused, a faraway look in his eye. "From a small Wyandot, who is the best man I ever knew. He may be dead by now, but somehow I don't think so."

Pumpkin slung his small gathering bag over his shoulder and headed out to make another false trail. "I had a dream two nights ago," he said. "There was a man in the dream. He talked in the Shemanese tongue. Maybe he's the one you're talking about, father."

"That may be son."

"I don't think so though. That man had only one good arm."

*     *     *

The men of Dancer's small village were quick to follow the plan their "king" had laid out for them. To a few of the young Kickapoos it seemed almost a game of hide and seek. The women however had no such delusions. Their lives, difficult at best, would be made much harder in the coming days. Some of their precious cooking equipment would have to be left behind in order to give credence to their plan to deceive the Otoes. No longer would they be warmed by a central fire in their lodges, but would find themselves struggling just to keep their children from freezing to death in the wilderness. For the women it was not a game!

"Father," Pumpkin said, pulling at Dancer's legging, "do you still have my 'snow snake'* pole?"

"Not now Pumpkin. All of us are very busy. We must be ready to leave very soon. I don't even know where that thing is. Besides, there is no snow on the ground anyway."

"What are you talking about?" Council Speaker demanded. "Why do you waste time talking with the boy about a game?There is much that we need to decide and much that still needs to be done!"

Pumpkin pulled on his father's tunic again. "There will be a snow. A great big snow too!" he said with a happy smile.

Dancer turned from his Head Elder and stared at the boy. "Are you sure of this my son? Are you very sure? It is only the 'moon of hunters', too early for snow. If you are right we may need to postpone our plans to escape."

Council Speaker, who had heard the entire conversation, was livid. "What is this? Why do you even listen to the words of a child of less than six or seven winters? There will be no snow!"

* "Snow snake" was a winter game played by children and young adults of many tribes. A carefully chosen sapling was smoothed and polished to facilitate its flight along a prepared, grooved path in the snow. The player would run forward and send the "snake" sliding along. Bets were taken regarding which pole would travel the farthest. Amazing distances by better players have been recorded.

"It is not yet even winter. Also my knees are not hurting. They always ache before a snow comes. Tell your boy to go and help his mother. We elders will not be ruled by the whims of a child. Pumpkin is <u>wrong</u>!" He strutted away.

Dancer King was troubled. He was beginning to trust the boy's 'second sight', but what if this time it was not true? Their plans were made. The sun was rising above the treetops. The sky was clear, not a cloud in view. There was no wind. With a sigh he called the Council Speaker back. "We leave as planned," he said. The Elder grunted his reluctant agreement.

*    *    *

Wisely, Dancer King hadn't called a general council meeting on this, their day of departure. Each clan member had been carefully taught where and how they were to scatter, and where to rejoin, a day's journey to the north. Fast and easy travel on the well-worn river trail had been expressly forbidden by the Dancer, as the Otoe would assume it would be the route the Kickapoo would take.

"See it? See it Father?" Pumpkin said, pointing to a roll of low-lying clouds which had suddenly been forming in the west. "Snow-maker comes! Did I do well? Did I?"

"You did, my son! Now you must see to your youngest sister. Keep her close to you and her mother. If she cannot walk fast enough you must put her on your back and carry her. Be very careful as you make your way through the brush. There will be no trail to follow. Do not <u>ever</u> lose sight of the others ahead of you."

"But I don't know if I can . . ."

Dancer ignored the protest, nodded to Polly and all of them, then left the lodge. Tears were shed, but Polly, following the plan, headed toward the gardens while Beth and her older daughter led Pumpkin and the four-year-old to the berry patches. Others could be seen moving off in all directions, deliberately leaving a few moccasin tracks here and there, even though it appeared likely that all tracks would soon be covered by snow.

Fingers of smoke rose from the tops of three lodges and the aroma of hot food wafted its way throughout the village. As planned, the clearing appeared no different than it would have on any other fall morning.

Dancer made one last look around, checking for anything that might give them away. He raised a hand to Ta-Kwa-no, who was seated before his family's lodge. The fastest runner in the clan, the lad had been chosen for the dangerous job of remaining behind, should the Otoes make a surprise attack on their village. If they did come, he was to delay them as long as possible, then run to the rendezvous in the forest.

Ta-Kwa-no did not acknowledge Dancer's raised hand, but sat down, pretending to straightens an arrow shaft over a large fire. His dog sat nearby, occasionally raising its muzzle to shake off a few snowflakes.

Dancer left them, heading for the river trail where he had placed the bird skull which He Sees had given them.

A little after mid-day the young Otoe, Climber, walked his pony north along the river trail. His two companions followed, riding double on a tired-looking mare. Climber's big white horse suddenly planted his front hooves and shied sideways a step or two. Climber leaned over the horse's neck to see what had made the horse so nervous. The rock pile and bird skull took up much of the narrow pathway. Alarmed, the young brave studied the apparition before him.

"What's wrong? Why did you stop like that?" one of the boys asked, trying to peer over the horse before him.

"It's . . . it's a sign! Get down and help me see what it means."

All three crowded closer, keeping a tight hand on their mounts' bridles. "Aieee!" one of them hissed. "Do not go any closer. It is a conjure! I think it means we should go no further north on this trail!"

Climber took another step closer. The others gasped at such foolishness. Their leader spent another minute studying the object, and more particularly the sandy soil around it. "Look here!" he exclaimed. Only the finest tracker would have noticed the tiny depression just off the trail. "Look friends, what do you see?"

The other two saw nothing except the ugly skull facing them. Climber pointed dramatically, a superior smile on his face. They saw it then, just off the trail the toe of a moccasin had left the smallest impression.

"Cowards!" their leader berated them. "This is nothing but a <u>trick</u>. I've been watching for just this sort of thing the foolish Kickapoos would try. They meant to slow down our pursuit, but this is proof that our quarry is moving north." The young man kicked the skull into the bushes and scattered the pile of rocks. "Nan-tadeo, Mount up behind me. Red Hand, ride back to our village. Tell Looks Back that Dancer King and his village have left their camp!"

"But Climber, I think we should be sure before we make such a report. Their camp is not far. Why not creep close and see if any of the Kickapoos are still here?"

"May Manitou deliver me from companions who act like old women!" Climber sighed. "Very well, it shouldn't take long, Come on."

With Climber leading they left the river trail and silently approached Dancer's camp. When the five lodges were in sight they crept forward, careful to stay hidden.

"See," Nan-tadeo whispered, "they are still here. The women are preparing food. Smoke from their cooking fires rises from those two lodges over there. See, I <u>told</u> you we should make sure before we deliver our report!"

Climber gave his friend a look of contempt. "Of course we can see smoke. A little <u>too</u> <u>much</u> smoke, don't you think?"

"But don't you see that boy sitting in front of his lodge? And that must be his dog with him." Climber's other companion argued.

"Of course I see that wegta [youth]! He has been sitting by that fire and pretending to straighten an arrow shaft ever since we slipped up here. What kind of fire is used when working a crooked shaft?"

"A <u>small</u> fire," his friend agreed, frowning.

"And why would he sit out in the falling snow? He could do that work inside. They have left their homes, I'm sure of it. All that we see before us is but a ruse. The smoke, the conjure skull on the trail, and even this boy and his dog. Dancer King's people have escaped!" Climber hissed.

At that moment the boy's dog suddenly stood up, hackles on his back bristling.

"The dog has caught our scent!" Red Hand whispered. "Should we go back before the boy sees us?"

"No. We will parlay with that wegta. It should be amusing. I'll go first. You two follow, one at a time."

Climber rose from their hiding place and stepped boldly into the clearing. "Ah ty!" he shouted.

The dog's lips drew back from his teeth, a low growl rumbling in its chest. "Ah ty!" Climber greeted the boy again. "If that ugly cur tries to attack I will kill it with my lance."

"Good greeting," the Kickapoo replied in sign language. He slapped his dog on the ears and held it by one leg.

"You need not sign to me. My friends and I know a little of your language. Now, where are all the people?"

"They . . . they . . . . they are . . . I mean all over! They're all over. Some in the gardens, some berrying, others . . . you know . . ."

"Why do you tremble so? Are you afraid of us?" Red Hand demanded.

"No. . . . I'm not afraid . . .I . . . Would you like some food? I'll get food. The women are getting food ready. Just let me go inside and get . . ."

"There is no need. We will come in and sit by the fire."

"No. That would not be good. We have the sickness in our lodge. I will bring food out."

For the first time the Otoes were uncertain. Perhaps it was true. After all, that was what Rattler and the Otoe Elders were saying. "Let him bring the food," Red Hand said hurriedly. "We will wait out here."

"That is good. I'll take my dog inside with me to be sure he doesn't cause you harm. Seat yourselves by my fire. I will not be long."

Ta-Kwa-no dragged his dog inside, careful to let the door flap fall in place behind them. With one hand he rattled a copper kettle and with the other, slipped a rawhide leash over the dog's head. He slung a small pack over his shoulder and with a quick, sad look around, slipped through a crack in the back wall. The concealed escape opening had been Council Speaker's idea, and a brilliant one it was.

The boy ran hard, avoiding all paths and game trails. Sometimes he was nearly dragging the big dog, which wanted to go back and guard the lodge. Ta-Kwa-no was tempted to remove the leash, but knew he must get much farther away before the animal would stay near him.

A chill ran through him as he heard an angry shout. They had circled the lodge and found the opening! The Otoe boys would be following his tracks now!

"We should go back and tell Looks Back right now!" Red Hand growled, having lost the track yet again.

"Nonsense!" Climber panted. "We will find the cowardly Kickapoos and confront them! When they see that they have been discovered they will return with their heads hanging!"

"We will be heroes!" the youngest boy cried. "All will praise us that the work of skinning and butchering the buffalo will be done by the people of him who calls himself a king."

"You are right!" Climber exclaimed, clapping a hand on his friend's shoulder. "And after our great hunt in the flatlands to the west, the 'king' and his people will be given the 'honor' of carrying all the meat back to our town! Ha ha!"

"I still think we should go back before . . ."

"Quiet, 'old woman'!" Climber growled. "We will soon strike the trail of those who are running away. After all, how could a whole group of people conceal their passage?"

Ta-Kwa-no altered his route to make sure he came to the garden plots. He picked up the heavy dog and mingled his own footprints with those made by the women early that morning. He re-settled his small pack, made up of a doeskin rolled up around a few items of food. The snow was falling heavier by the minute.

Back in the forest he released the dog . Unencumbered, he fairly flew to the north. Now it was plain to see why he alone had been chosen to remain in the camp. Tall and thin, his physique was made for running. Nothing slowed his flight. The occasional brier patch he skirted with hardly a change of pace. Logs, roots, none was an impediment.

By this time Ta-Kwa-no felt confident that if anyone still followed they could never catch him. He slowed to a walk then finally stopped altogether. Seated on a log, he unfastened the bedroll and draped it over his head for protection from the snow. He ate a handful of parched corn. The dog begged for a few kernels, but the lad gave him none. Who could say how long it might be until he could re-join the clan?

Rested somewhat, he tried running and walking again, but after falling twice in the deepening snow, gave it up. Using sticks and branches Ta-Kwa-no fashioned a crude lean-to. At first he used the doeskin for a roof but the wind was rising and he was not dressed for the cold. He pulled the robe down, shook off the snow, and wrapped up in it, but was too cold to sleep. "They told me," he thought. "Pumpkin said I should take warm clothes, but I didn't believe him, and anyway it would have slowed me down."

The night was barely half over when the boy was startled by the crash of a falling tree. By now the wind was howling, blowing the snow sideways. He was chilled to the bone, and his feet were becoming numb. The dog! He must find the dog, but the darkness and blowing snow made this impossible. Then, at that moment, the big dog rose from the nest it had made, shook off the snow, and crept against his master's body. They lay there shivering until the weak light of a snow-filled dawn finally arrived.

Boy and dog stared in amazement. Everything had changed. The snow lay knee deep everywhere, and it continued to fall. Drifts were forming behind every rock and tree. The wind had not diminished.

For the first time since he had raced away from the Otoe boys, Ta-Kwa-no felt real fear. He hadn't worn heavy leggings nor winter moccasins, knowing that those would have slowed his running. He and his dog had no idea exactly where they were or how far they still must travel to find the rest of Dancer's band. He didn't even know which way was north!

Both boy and animal were cold and hungry. The creature nuzzled his master and whined uncertainly. "I know. I know! It's cold and the snow is deep, but we must get out from under this robe and find the others. May Manitou help us!"

He stood up, brushed the snow from the robe, and tried to determine which direction was north. The sun was not visible, and the snow had made it impossible to see moss on tree trunks. Once more, fear held him in an icy grip.

Perhaps Manitou had heard his prayer, for suddenly Blackie shook himself mightily and started away.

"Ah, so!" the boy shouted. "You want to go back to our village do you? Well now I am sure. We must go the other way!" He called the dog, slipped a leash around its neck, and they headed north.

At first they made slow progress. The wind had abated a little, but because of the snowdrifts and hidden obstructions beneath them it was nearly impossible to maintain a straight line of travel. What was more alarming was the fact that the boy's feet were now completely numb.

Ta-Kwa-no was exhausted. Plowing through knee deep snow, falling over hidden logs and roots, and battling the wind had all taken their toll. A growing boy, he was hungry and thirsty.

"I know what you always told me, Grandfather, but I can't help it. I'll eat some snow, just a little, then at least I won't be so thirsty anymore."

As was the custom, the grandfather had taken over his training two years before. The man had stressed that eating snow was never wise. "Always take time to make fire and melt some snow. The warm water will then help you. Eating cold snow will only give you 'the chills'."

"I remember Grandfather but I have nothing to make fire with," the lad said aloud. His mind was beginning to play tricks.

A deer, sheltering under the low branches of a fir tree, suddenly burst forth in a shower of snow. Ta-Kwa-no, staggering forward, hardly noticed. His dog did notice! Yanking the leash from the boy's hand, he bounded away in pursuit. The lad tried to whistle him back, but his lips were beginning to freeze.

"I must rest! If I just rest for a few minutes I will be able to keep going, Grandfather".

"No! Do not stop! If you do . . ."

He slid forward into a snow bank, and lay still. "How warm the snow is!" he told the old man standing beside him. "I will only sleep for a few heartbeats. Are you warm enough? You don't have warm clothing. You are <u>old</u>. You shouldn't be out in this weather. Lie down beside me. I'll keep you safe in this warm snow."

The dog finally lurched its way back from the unsuccessful pursuit. It licked the boy's face, then curled up beside him.

Some time later the animal did all it could to alert his master but nothing helped. At last it turned and with a mournful whine, headed back toward the camp it had always known as its home.

*       *       *

"I can't carry her anymore. I have to sit down now. Why can't she walk like the rest of us? Help me, mother!"

Polly called to Dancer. "We must stop now, my husband! We <u>must</u>! The snow has made the walking terrible. Pumpkin cannot continue carrying Beth's youngest one. And look, old Badger is falling farther and farther behind. He will die if we don't stop soon."

Dancer King slogged back through the drifts and joined her. "Elders! Elders!" he called. "We stop for a short rest. You have all done well, breaking trail ahead of us. Wives, make fire. Melt snow for soogartea."

"We have no sugar for the drink," Council Speaker complained. "You made us leave it behind when we were planning this foolish escape at the beginning of winter."

"Ah, but I <u>have</u> some!" Dancer crowed. "Not much, but enough for a little for each of you." He pulled a small pouch from beneath his tunic and handed it to Polly.

Council Speaker was not mollified. "This snow will make it impossible for us to reach the Arikara people before we all die of the cold," he growled. "I've been talking to the other Elders. We agree that we should go back where we belong. Back to our warm lodges, our gardens, our . . ."

"Go <u>back</u>?" Dancer exploded. "You know as well as I that the Otoes intend to make <u>slaves</u> of us!"

"Better a live slave than a frozen corpse!" Council Speaker looked around the fire. Several were nodding in agreement. "You, Dancer King, are just afraid of being forced to work for a change. I don't see what is so terrible about slavery anyway. Food, shelter, friends, what more could anyone ask?"

"You are forgetting one thing, Council Speaker. Not only would the Otoes enslave us, but He Sees told us that his people would kill the old and the very young of our clan. Even many of those who are healthy would likely die on the trail to the buffalo lands. Look Back's people will be mounted on fine horses. How many horses do we have?"

No one, including Council Speaker, could answer that question. Still grumbling, he joined the other Elders standing around the fire.

"We must not tarry much longer," Dancer said. "We have a long trail ahead of us. Perhaps the snow will be gone in a few . . ."

"<u>Father</u>!" Pumpkin suddenly interrupted.

"No, my son, there is little time. We must . . ."

The lad turned slowly to face Dancer King. A strange expression seemed to set his face like flint. "You will <u>hear</u> me!" Handing his empty trade cup to his mother the boy faced the north and pointed. "Shemanese!" he exclaimed.

"What? What is this? Polly, take charge of your son. He is talking nonsense."

"<u>My</u> <u>son</u> is it?" the woman cried. "He is more yours than mine. From you he has been given 'the gift'. Listen to what he says!"

"Shemanese in the forest," the boy repeated quietly.

"I've heard about all I care to hear from this wonderful 'gifted' boy!" Council Speaker uttered contemptuously. "Look at him. He's not even a pure-blood. How could he be . . ."

"Stop it!" Beth told him, gathering her nephew close to her side. "My sister's son <u>does</u> have 'the gift'! You will see." The boy had started to cry.

"Yes! We'll see alright. We should not even be listening to this half-breed. He's nothing but a . . ."

"<u>Hello</u> <u>the</u> <u>camp</u>!" A voice echoed faintly through the trees. "Anybody down there?"

"Aw, stop it Joe. Even if they was, they can't understand our lingo. Watch this. <u>Who</u> <u>are</u> <u>ya</u>?" he yelled. "We smelled your smoke, but whoever you are, you don't know what . . ."

"We'uns is over <u>here</u>!" Dancer shouted in English. "Come on into our camp. Please hurry youselfs. We is cold and hongry!"

"Well what do ya think of that, Joe?" he asked, slogging forward. "How in blazes is there gennywine Americans way out here in all these big woods? Why lookee there, Joe. They're just hunkered down in the snow. No wonder they're cold. Got kids with 'em too. If this don't beat all!"

"Brady, look. Ain't he a <u>black</u> man?"

"He shore is. Prolly a runaway slave as has took up with this bunch of Injuns. Who talks real English?" he yelled as they neared the fire.

"I does. My name's Simon, but some calls me Dancer. I be sort of a headman of these hyar peoples."

"You? A <u>darkey</u>? How'd that come to be mister? But before you get to palaverin' on that there, we'd like to buy some food from you. We been out cheer a day and a night. Durn storm come up on us mighty sudden. Near froze me and my cousin here to death."

"Quiet Joe. We need to find out what's what with all these folks. Well, Dancer Man, what's yore story? And mind ya it better be the truth." He shifted his rifle to the other hand, making sure they saw the weapon.

"Yawl fine gennelmans come on in here to our settin' place,"Dancer drawled. "Weuns ain't got hardly no food though, but we is gwine to share as to what we do got."

Dancer's wives and son were not surprised by his manner of speaking to the two white visitors. They had seen him make this instant dialectic change on many occasions as they made their way west. Any former slave who had managed to escape from his former master could never tell when they might be exposed. It was always best to appear the ignorant, subservient "darkey" until any danger appeared to be past.

"Well mister, what in tarnation are you folks doin' way out here next to nowheres?"

Dancer briefly explained their circumstances, but it was soon apparent that the white men had little interest. "You say you're headin' for them Arikara devils?" Joe asked. "Why that would take you prolly another week, walkin' like you folks is!"

The Kickapoos were shocked. None of them had actually known how far north the Arikara lands were located, or how long it would take to get there.

Seeing their looks of pain and hopelessness, Brady, somewhat uncharacteristically, had a suggestion. "Seein' as how any fool can tell you'd never make it that far, why don't youns just come on to old Lisa's camp with us. I reckon he'd be willing to give you a little food till you figger out what to do. 'Course," he added hurriedly, "Joe and me can't speak for the Captain. Not atall we cain't!"

"Thank you! That would suit us just fine," Dancer said eagerly. [The "poor, ignorant darkey" speech patterns had disappeared!] "We can be ready to follow you right now. Settin' here has made us all colder than we was before. Lead the way. Our men will take turns with you breaking trail."

Joe and Brady glanced at each other. With a guilty look, Joe spoke up. "The truth is mister, Brady and me, we don't have no idea whereat's the fur tradin' camp!"

The moment Dancer had finished translating there were looks of astonishment which quickly changed to grief and despair. Beth's girls burst into tears.

"We was to do some huntin' for Manuel Lisa's camp, but like I said, we was caught in the storm. Seems like we got all mixed up some way or other. We been sloggin' around all day, trying to find our way, but . . . well, like I said, we're <u>lost</u>!"

Joe stared off toward the west. "It's thataway Brady," he said, pointing. "I'm sure it is."

"Wait, we dare not leave yet!" one of the women shouted. "Ta-Kwa-no has not joined up with us. He will certainly be coming soon."

"But he would have no trouble following our trail through the snow. The two white men are anxious to leave. Without them to speak for us we would certainly be unwelcome at the fur traders' camp," Council Speaker argued.

"He is my <u>son</u>!" one of the Elders cried. "We cannot just go and leave him, wherever he is!"

Council Speaker stood face-to-face with the Dancer King. "There is little time," he said, not unkindly. "You are our leader. Now you must make the decision. Do we wait here with little food and no protection from the storm? The little ones, your daughters and your son Ripe Pumpkin among them, are cold, hungry and exhausted. Night will soon be upon us. If we wait for Ta-Kwa-no much longer we will not have the Shemanese to help break trail. Some of our little band will surely die."

Dancer fought down the urge to lash out at the man. "I have enjoyed being their 'king'," he thought. "No work, food brought to me, looked up to by nearly everyone . . . So it appears that now I must act like a <u>real</u> king. No matter how I rule, someone, maybe several of us will surely die."

"Well?"

Dancer had completely forgotten his best Elder, who was still facing him, demanding an answer. "Everyone up!" he finally commanded, using what he hoped was a kingly voice. "Joe and Brady, lead the way."

Pumpkin hurried up to his parents, dragging Beth's youngest by the hand. "Why father?" he asked.

"What do you mean, Pun kie . . . I mean Pumpkin?"

"How did you decide what we should do?"

Dancer looked at the boy's mother, eyes wide in astonishment. "Did you hear that?" he asked her. "What sort of child would ask such a thing?"

"Ask <u>him</u> then. He can answer for himself."

Stumbling through the snow and half carrying his little sister, the boy retorted "I need to learn how to . . . I mean . . . how to <u>decide</u> things."

Dancer swung the little girl to his shoulders so Pumpkin could come closer and hear better. "It was not easy my son. Deciding important things never is. But this is how I knew what had to be done; it is possible that Ta-Kwa-no will not be able to find us. He may die. But if we don't follow the two Shemanese to their camp it is likely that several will die. It is usually right to do what is <u>best</u> for the <u>most</u>. Do you understand what I'm telling you?"

"Yes father. I can see that it's easy if you just figure out what's best for a whole lot of people! Thank you Pa-Pa."

"Don't make a mistake here, Pumpkin. Remember I said it is <u>usually</u> right to do the best for the most. Sometimes though, there might be one person who has a better idea, or a better plan than all the others put together. Then is the time when it will take all your strength and all your good sense to make a right decision. Do you understand what I'm telling you?"

The boy stood stock still, completely oblivious to those pushing through the snow around them. His lower lip began to quiver as he answered. "No Pa-pa, I don't understand all of what you just said."

They began walking again. "Well first of all it will take years until you can completely understand. Some grown-ups never do! Let me give you an example. Maybe that will help you. Let's pretend that all of these people around us are slave owners. Let's say that they all like to keep slaves. But your father, that's me, Punkie, hates slavery. Many say that owning someone is a good thing, but I say it isn't. Who would be right, my son?" He paused to brush the snow from Pumpkin's hood.

Pumpkin dropped to his knees in the snow and threw his arms around Dancer's legs, "<u>You</u> would be father! You would be right! Do you have any maple candy left?"

Dancer King laughed aloud. He patted the boy's back and pushed him forward again.

"Father, I will tell you now that Ta-Kwa-no is already dead. So you made the right decide."

"What do you <u>mean</u>?" Polly gasped. She would have stopped walking, but Dancer pushed her forward. They must keep moving!

"I saw him. He went to sleep in the snow. Then I saw him walking."

Polly was confused. "If he was walking, then he must be alive."

"You don't believe me!" A tear slid down the boy's cheek. "Why do I have to <u>see</u> <u>things</u>?" he cried. "I don't <u>want</u> to see things anymore!"

"But if he was walking . . ."

"He was walking <u>up in the sky</u>!" Pumpkin sobbed.

Dancer grabbed the boy's arm and pulled him close. "I believe you," he said. "But why didn't you tell me sooner?"

"I waited because I wanted to learn how to decide things. Now father you must help me catch up to the two white men. They are leading us in the wrong way."

"What do ya <u>mean</u>?" Joe snarled when the boy and his father reached them. "You tryin' to tell me this kid here  knows the way back to Lisa's camp better'n me and Brady does? Why you'uns ain't never even been there!"

Council Speaker kicked his way through he snow to Dancer at the head of the line of straggling movers. "Why have they stopped to argue?"

"Pumpkin has told them they are leading us in the wrong direction. They don't believe that this little boy could possibly know the way better than they do."

"Ah, so! Tell those two Shemanese that your son <u>knows</u>!" Council Speaker exploded. "He has <u>the sight</u>! Tell them Dancer!"

Dancer hid a grin and lifted his son to a shoulder.

Pumpkin calmly pointed out the correct direction.

Well before sundown, Brady, Joe, and the Dancer King's clan stumbled gratefully into Manuel Lisa's trading camp.

*　　　　　　*　　　　　　*

"So you are finally back! Where have you been anyway?" Captain Lisa was angry. He didn't like to be kept waiting.

Tom however, still breathing hard from he and Joe's difficult run through the snow-choked forest, hardly noticed. He slid to a sitting position against the tent wall. This lack of respect further fed Lisa's anger, but still Toom-She-chi-Kwa said nothing.

"Listen to me. I've offered you a high position in my organization. I've yet to hear a word of thanks. What you would have done had I not taken you on I cannot imagine. Now I will hear you speak!"

Tom looked up at the man standing before him, feet wide and arms folded. He shook his head for a moment, then said, "I am grateful Monsieur, and you are right, I had no other place to go. But you must understand my grief. With my wife, Menseeta, it was not like some Indian marriages, and some white marriages too. I truly loved her. I did! And now your instant justice has torn her from me. Also . . ."

"Enough!" the Captain snapped. "What would you have done were the decision up to you? I have heard that as a lad you spent some years with a Quaker family. I have the highest regard for persons of that faith, although admittedly I find some of their customs a little strange. What did you learn from them, Tom Bluefoot?"

Tom had to respect the Spanish-American's cleverness.

"I learned to tell the truth."

"And that is not all they taught you is it? You see, two years ago I spent almost a month in a Quaker mission, recovering from an illness. Truthfulness was a virtue they stressed, but there were two others also. What were they? You tell me!"

Tom stood up and faced this intelligent leader of men. "Peace and selflessness," he sighed.

"Tell me what is meant by selflessness." Of course Lisa already knew the answer.

"It means placing the well-being of others ahead of your own. You are a clever man, Manuel Lisa! You've made me see that leaving my wife and daughter with the Frenchman was the right thing to do. There is no way that I can provide for them, especially out here in the wilderness. Thank you! I will do my best to be a good interpreter for you."

"That is what I wanted to hear."

Tom tried to straighten up a little. "But still," he added, "it will be a long trail for me, living so close, but having no claim to them."

"Yes. Yes it will. Now go and find Jack Meeks. He will see that you have food and proper clothing. We may try to leave tomorrow if this blasted snow ever stops. You may sleep against that wall in my tent. Tell Jack that he is to give you a buffalo robe. You will need it, as it appears that winter has come early to . . ."

Lisa's servant burst into the tent dragging snow with her. "Peoples come! <u>Many</u> peoples. They come. Hungry, cold. Brady and Joe come! Brady and Joe come along peoples!" she shouted.

"Where are they now, Birdsong?" Lisa asked, shrugging into his heavy coat. He followed the Indian woman out into the snow that continued to fall.

The large tent seemed empty without the commanding presence of their expedition leader. For a moment no one spoke. The arrival of the unknown travelers meant little to them, as there were already over fifty in Lisa's employ.

"Father! Father listen to me. I am here. Also Tadpole who was your . . . I mean . . . I mean my mother is with us too. . You must not blame my mother or me. You were gone, maybe five winters. We did all we could to stay alive. I cleaned some Shemanese houses for silver money, but Mama made me stop because . . . well because . . . some of the Shemanese men and older boys were after me. Mama made shirts and moccasins and we decorated them with quills. We stayed alive, but we were always hungry. Cold Maker was a bad visitor in our flimsy lodge. Then Phillipe came. He made us work hard for him, but mainly he was good to us. He became my Pa-Pa' but I never forgot you! I felt that some day we would see you again. Now . . ."

"Cattail! My little Cattail!" Tom cried, standing to embrace his daughter. "It has been long! So very, very long!" He pushed her back so the light from the central fire lighted her face. "You are all grown up!" he breathed. "And so beautiful!"

"Yes Pa-Pa. Manuel calls me 'Forest Flower'. He seems to like me."

"I am also here, my husband. I am here, Cattail is here, and you are here." Tom, so taken by his daughter, had not noticed Menseeta's silent approach.

"We must let the many summers and winters behind us remain only in what our hearts hold to. Cattail [she refused to call her daughter by the new name Captain Lisa had given her] is right. We are here. Together. Manitou has done this, or perhaps the Shemanese three-part God. Who can say?"

"I don't know what to say to you now," Tom moaned. "It must be that you are not my wife anymore."

"Do not blame Captain Lisa. He had to make the final decision since I could not do it!"

"I don't blame him, but my heart is torn almost as bad as this useless arm. Monsieur Lisa was right, but I say it again, I grieve for my wife and daughter."

Cattail touched her father's arm. "But we will be traveling together. We can be friends at least."

Toom-She-chi-Kwa was not convinced. "I will do my best, if he [Tom glanced at Philippe, who had not come near] will do the same. But I'm afraid that it will be . . ."

The door flap swept open, bringing a swirl of snow. "Ah, what a storm!" Lisa said, shaking snow onto the earthen floor. "There must be twenty or more of those people!" he fumed. "I should have known better than to send those two bumblers out to hunt. They brought back no meat, but rather a crowd of hungry, half-frozen Kickapoos. May the devil take Joe and Brady!"

Hardly had the Indian servant re-fastened the heavy buffalo-skin door flap when it was yanked open again. Some snow blew in, but it was obvious that the wind and storm was finally abating. "What now?" Lisa practically shouted. "Someone hold that blasted robe shut. It's freezing in here!"

"Sorry Captain, but these men wouldn't have it no other way than to bust in on you and . . . and these others in here."

'Fritz," Lisa said disgustedly, "you are one of my best men, but if you have no better sense than to . . ."

"It's our fault yer honor. Don't blame the Dutchy here. We <u>made</u> him bring us, me and Brady, and the kid here."

For the first time Manuel Lisa noticed a small child, so bundled in borrowed robes and furs as to be nearly invisible. Intrigued, he nodded for Brady to bring him closer. "Why did you bring this little one to my tent?"

Joe drew himself up, took the child's hand and marched him up to the table. "This here's the ding-dongest kid you ever laid eyes on, Captain. You see. . ."

"Never mind that. What I need to hear from you two right now is where in blazes have you two been for two days? And where's the venison you bragged about bringing in?"

"Beggin' yer pardon Sir, but I'm Joe. He's Brady right there. Now about this here youngun."

"So, <u>Joe</u>," he emphasized the name with heavy sarcasm, "I asked you explain your absence. Get to it!"

"It were the storm yer hon . . . uh, Captain. Me and Brady was just about to get you the biggest, fattest old black bear you ever seen when <u>bam</u>! That snowstorm hit us like a thousand of brick!"

"A black bear you say?"

"Shore enough. A big one too."

"Strange," Lisa said, sneering a little. "Black bears den up for the winter early out here. Wonder why that one was still out?"

"Aw fergit that Joe. You never was no kind of a good liar," Brady said. "Captain, here's the straight of it. We got plumb losted after that blizzard struck. Why you couldn't see <u>nothing</u>. Never saw the sun till near dark yesterday, so couldn't get our directions straight. Not atall we couldn't."

"Well that I can understand. We were hit here too. Actually you were lucky because I had planned to head west, but decided to wait until this blasted unusual weather cleared. Otherwise we would have been gone upriver. You and those Indians who came with you would certainly have perished . Now what about this child? Is he sick?"

"Oh no," Brady continued. "This here little Injun is the one who saved all our lives!"

Captain Lisa rolled his eyes and groaned. "Is this another 'bear story' from you two?"

Pumpkin had neither spoken nor moved during all of this. Joe helped the boy untangle from all his wraps, then said, "Here he is Captain. His name means Punkin or somethin' like that."

Manuel Lisa extended a hand and was surprised when the boy took it immediately. "Pumpkin is it? How old are you my boy? Oh I'm sorry, you can't understand me can you?"

"Yassuh, yassuh, yassuh!" Pumpkin replied.

Lisa looked at Brady and Joe in astonishment. "Does he speak English then?"

"Yassuh, yassuh, yassuh!" Joe cackled. Lisa was not amused. "He kin talk it alright but he learnt it from his daddy who's a black man. I reckon you've heard lots of that kinda talk down there in New Orleans where I heard you come from."

"Indeed, indeed. Has the child been fed? And the others?"

"All took care of yer honor. Yer men's been good to take 'em into their tents, even so there was lots of cussin' while they was doin' it. Haw haw!"

"An exceedingly handsome child. I can see that he is no full-blood, but then again he doesn't resemble a half-breed either. Curious. But I do not understand why you've brought him to me. He should be sleeping lest he catch a chill."

"This here is the best part. Like I said he saved us all. The whole kit and kaboodle of usns."

Lisa sat the boy on his lap and studied him closely. He was amazed again when Pumpkin looked directly back at him, a complete stranger, with no fear, only interest. "How could this boy save you or anyone? He must be no more than ten years old."

Pumpkin held up six fingers. Captain Lisa laughed aloud, completely charmed by a child he had known for less than fifteen minutes.

Tom Bluefoot, lost in a cloud of hopelessness and self-pity, paid no attention to anything happening nearby, but when he heard Lisa's laughter, a very rare happening, he looked up.

The boy still sat on the Captain's lap, a huge grin showing two missing front teeth. Something about the child struck a chord deep in Tom's mind. He shrugged it off.

"Now Brady or Joe, whichever one you are, how did this cute little fellow, who is falling asleep, manage to save your mostly worthless lives?"

"Well sir, like I said we got lost in the storm. We was wallerin' around in the snow tryin' to figure the way back here. Truth to tell, we was headin' about ten degrees west of the way we oughta be goin'. Punkin here, he just pointed the right way. Said he heard 'white people talk' but we was maybe ten miles from yer camp! They say this kid has some kind of 'gift'. Maybe he does. What do you think?"

"What of his parents? Are either one or both of them with the rest that followed you men in tonight?"

"Now I'll tell you about them sir. You see," he began pontifically, "as yawl kin see, the kid don't look like no half-breed. Leastaways none I ever seen."

"Just get to the point, Joe! What do you know about his parents? You'll notice I said what do <u>you know</u> not what you <u>think</u>!"

"Joe's right, Captain Lisa. Pumpkin's ma is a squaw, Wyandot I think they said. But, and here's the funny thing, his daddy's a darkey! Likely a runaway slave. We saw lots of 'em when we was comin' out here this way out of Ohio Territory."

Joe butted in. "You'll have to meet up with that black man Sir. He says [Joe chuckled a little] he says he's a king! He musta bamboozled some tribe into believin' he's a real king. 'Dancer King' he call hisself. Why you never heard of such a thing!"

Tom leaped to his feet, nearly upsetting Lisa's prize folding table. "What did you say his name was?" he demanded. "Was it really 'Dancer'?"

"That's what he said mister. Why you gettin' all het up fer? He's probly sleepin' by now, just like all them others is. Truth be known, me and Joe needs to bed down ourselfs pretty soon. Little Pumpkin there on the Captain's lap is sleepin' already."

Awkwardly Tom struggled to pull a coat over his one bad arm. Without another word he yanked the door curtain open and dashed away in the darkness. Soon he could be heard shouting, "Simon! Simon! Where are you?"

"<u>Shut</u> <u>up</u> you!" a trapper yelled, his bellow waking more than Tom's shouting. "There's Indians bedded down all over this camp. So just quit yer yelling and go back to sleep!"

"Simon! <u>Simon</u>! It's me, Tom Bluefoot! I'm <u>here</u>! How did you ever . . ."

"Tom! Is that really you?" a voice called from the next tent. "Hold on! I'm a-comin' out, soon as get out from under this robe. Just hold on for a minute."

Complaints erupted as Dancer King crawled out from under the buffalo robe, lit a candle, and staggered out of the tent. "Where you at, Tom? Am I dreaming maybe?" He nearly fell in the heavy snow.

"It's me alright. Oh Simon, I can't tell you how glad I am to see you after all these years. We've got so much to talk about. Where can we go to get out of this cold?" They hugged each other desperately.

"Go <u>somewhere</u>, for crying out loud!" an angry voice came from the tent.

"Yeah! <u>Do</u> <u>that</u>!" another trapper shouted. "And Dancer Man, or whoever you are, fasten that blamed tent flap before we all freeze to death!"

"Come on," Tom whispered. "Lisa's big tent will be fine."

They managed to sneak into the spacious tent, found a corner, and sat as close together as possible. They talked almost non-stop for several hours.


"That's awful Tom. Just awful! Losing your wife and daughter like that. Just you go ahead and bawl yawl's eyes out. 'Tears washes away hurts' my old Granny allus told us younguns."

"I've been looking for you for a year and a half, Simon. Sometimes I thought I'd never find you and your family, but I felt like if I <u>could</u>, everything would work out just right. Now, even though I'm very glad to finally be re-united with you, my very best friend, everything has all gone to pieces for me."

"I knew we'd see each other again."

"I thought we might too, but . . ."

"No, I said I <u>knew</u>!" Dancer stated.

"You knew?"

"I sure as shootin' did. Pumpkin told us."

"Your son? I remember him as just a baby in a cradleboard a long time ago, back there in Green Ville."

"Yes, he has 'the gift'. He can sometimes tell what will happen in the future. Would you want me to ask him about your life in the years ahead?"

"No! I would rather not know."

"Me neither," Dancer chuckled. "But I have a favor to ask."

"Anything Simon. You know that. It would be good for both of us I think."

"Thank you Tom. Now I want to tell you this: we can plan all we want to, but that ain't always the way stuff turns out. Just do the best we can when the sun comes up ever mornin'! Now let's both just quit talkin'!"

Two hours later dawn found them both sound asleep.

As a Scottish poet would write centuries later, "The best laid plans of mice and men go oft astray!"

*                    *                    *

The morning of October seventeenth dawned to the most beautiful sight that could be experienced west of the Missouri River. Every tree, every bush, everything standing was coated and capped with a mantle of glistening white.

Manuel Lisa was in good spirits. He watched as the sun rose on the scene, adding even more beauty to the morning.

"Do we leave today?" Jason Nye, one of Lisa's most trusted advisers, asked his boss.

"Tomorrow," Manuel answered, finishing a cup of tea. "This early snow has certainly caused us a problem we did not expect. We'll use this day to get everything packed and ready. See to the boats. Have all our gear secure and ready for loading at first light. Anything else, Jason?"

"Yes Captain, there is. What about all those people who came in last night?"

"How many are there?"

"Brady said there was eighteen, Sir. Eleven men, four women, and three kids."

"What about the one who calls himself a king?" Lisa grinned. "Have you met him?"

"Only briefly, Captain," Jason Nye answered. "The whole bunch of them were pretty near exhausted last night. We fed them and bedded them down in different men's tents. That's about all I can say right now."

"Fine! Fine. What would I do without you, Jason? Find the black man. Have him come here as soon as possible. I'd like Brady and Joe here too, may heaven help me! Oh, one more thing. Be sure they bring the little boy they call Pumpkin. I'd like to see him again."

"Did yawl call my name, Captain?" A woolly head appeared from under a robe on the far wall. "I's right cheer!"

Lisa's tent, large though it was, seemed about to burst. To make more room the folding table and chairs had been removed and secured for loading. Everyone, even the Captain himself, had to sit on the floor.

The central fire provided more than enough heat for the many bodies crammed inside. The extra large central tent had been the inspiration of Manuel Lisa himself. He had rightly assumed that it would be very valuable for those times when the weather was too bad for trading in the open.

"Come in! Come in, all of you," Lisa boomed. "Seat yourselves close to the fire if you wish." Forest Flower was seated next to him on a folded robe.

Introductions were made, Tom Bluefoot kept busy interpreting. Phillipe had positioned himself as far from Tom as was possible, for which Toom-She-chi-Kwa was grateful. No one present was unaware of the significance of Cattail's position close to the Captain's left. [Menseeta, the girl's mother, most of all!] Phillipe however was elated!

"Now," Lisa began with a flashing smile, "so you are a king, are you? And just where is your kingdom located?" He expected Tom to translate, but there was no need.

"Oh no, no, no no! I'se jist a simple ol' darkey man as has come onto yawl's . . ."

Tom interrupted immediately. "There's no need for that act Simon. The Captain understands a great deal about slavery. Just be yourself."

"Mr. Bluefoot is correct, King Simon. Although my parents owned slaves I do not tolerate it here in the west. I pray to God that that awful situation will never sully the purity of this beautiful land. Tell me how you came to call yourself a king."

The black man showed his relief immediately.

"Actually Sir, some call me 'Dancer King'. I love to dance for anybody foolish enough to ask me. As for the 'king' part, well I sort of fooled a bunch of Kickapoos into thinking I could find them some free land way out here where the white people won't ever want to come. That way I could be safe too. So, here we is . . . I mean are."

"Very commendable. However I think the white people will come out this far too, now that we have purchased all this land from France. But that may not happen until long after your lifetime and mine." The Captain smiled his most charming smile. "Now I see you have brought the boy. Your son is he?"

"Yes Sir. We calls him Pumpkin. His Indian name is Sac-wea. We thought he was near the same color as a ripe pumpkin in the garden. He wasn't coppery like his ma nor black like me."

"And this fine lady is the boy's mother?"

"Yessir. This here's Polly. Now I gots another wife too. She's Polly's sister, Beth. She gots two little girls."

"Madam," Lisa said, "may I hold the boy for a little time? We must conclude here shortly. There is much still to do if all this crew can be on the river tomorrow."

"Pardon Suh," Dancer said, settling Pumpkin on Manuel Lisa's knee. "Since you brung it up, what's to become of all us folks? We had to light out mighty quick on account that them Otoes was meaning to attack and make slaves out of any of us they didn't kill off. I reckon we're safe from them now, since they've gone west to hunt buffalo. But Suh, we got nowhere to go, and we shore can't stay here once you're gone."

"That is why I have called you all here. My men and I have considered that issue with some concern. Here is what we propose: my best associate, Mr. Jason Nye, will stay with you at the river until a bateau comes along, heading downriver. They can take all of you aboard. As soon as . . ."

"Scuse me!" Dancer stammered. "We gots no money to pay our passage. And what about when we gets back to St. Louis or someplace?"

"Of course Dancer King. My man Jason will accompany you, carrying my letter of credit for all your expenses until you are back to wherever you wish to settle."

Everyone in the tent was stunned at such extravagance. "I don't know what to say to all of this! It's . . . it's jist powerful <u>powerful</u> nice out'n you Mr. Lisa," Dancer said, a tear sliding down one black cheek. Only a few of Lisa's associates were aware of the tremendous profits afforded by the fur trade.

"Captain." All were surprised to hear Tom Bluefoot's sudden interjection.

"Yes Mr. Bluefoot. What is it?" Lisa still held little Pumpkin. The child seemed perfectly content to remain there and watch what was going on.

"You might consider asking Dancer and his family to stay with your fur company as you head into the far west."

"Interesting," the Captain said. "And why do you suggest that?"

Tom was quick to reply. "As you undoubtedly know better than I, we Native Americans love ceremony. The Dancer was too modest. His dancing is very fine! The people you wish to engage in trade will love his performance as part of the opening ceremonies."

Never one to hesitate, the Captain turned little Pumpkin until the boy was looking up into his face. "What do <u>you</u> think, little man?" he asked. "Would you like to go on a long, hard trip and see all kinds of new things?"

"Yes. I will go. We will all come back before you are ready." His small clear words were met with shocked silence. Polly moved quickly to take the boy from Lisa's lap, but the Captain's nervous laughter finally defused the situation.

"You'd be smart to listen to the boy, Captain! I already told you how he got us goin' in the right direction, and . . ."

"Shut up Joe!" Brady hissed.

The tent emptied quietly. Manuel Lisa remained seated against the wall, frowning in concentration. What <u>was</u> it with this child? He glanced at Forest Flower, but she said nothing. And what did the boy mean by that statement?

\*            \*            \*

As quickly as it had come, the snow disappeared from the land. Manuel Lisa sat on a padded crate at the bow of the first keelboat. At his suggestion, Dancer, Tom Bluefoot, and one of his closest associates found seats nearby. Forest Flower, Polly and Pumpkin were enjoying a sort of make-shift cabin near the center of the craft. Beth, feeling that the long and possibly dangerous journey would be too much for her two little girls, had wisely chosen to wait for a boat back to St. Louis with the rest of the Kickapoos.

With every able-bodied man taking his turn at the poling, the three crafts had made steady progress into the virtually untouched territories of the Omaha, Ponca, Cheyenne and Pawnee. Even though volume had not been great, Lisa was pleased with the expedition's success. Hardly a week passed by until the flotilla was met with a delegation of friendly natives, anxious to barter furs, food, [and sometimes even <u>wives</u>] for the kettles, hatchets, and "foofuraw" jewelry they craved.

"Look at that darkey go!" Joe exclaimed, as Dancer did still another performance.

Including Dancer in his organization had indeed been the best decision Lisa could have made. Ever since Lewis and Clark's "Voyage of Discovery" some years before, the path was open for entrepreneurs bold enough [or foolish enough!] to venture forth.

Brady tried clapping along with the Dancer's self-accompaniment, but neither he nor his cousin could ever get it right. "Ya know," he said, giving up on the clapping, "when that old Omaha chief give him that rattle and the little drum he just natcherly got better and and better! And look how them squaws there keep givin' him the eye. Why they act near crazy about him!"

"Watch it Brady! You heard the Captain. He don't want us to call 'em squaws even though that's what they are sure enough."

None of the party [except possibly Pumpkin] had an inkling of what awaited them when four days later they tied up at the northern extent of the Arikara territory.

Dancer, enjoying his role as the main attraction, got ready. Over the years he had acquired an amazing variety of costume accouterments. Feathers, beads, hawk bells, and even bright yellow ribbons fluttered and tinkled as he approached the gangplank. He stopped in mid-stride and stared at the clearing. No one was there! He turned uncertainly to Captain Lisa. "Why Massa Lisa, suh, there ain't nobody as has come to trade. Maybe they didn't know we was comin'."

The Captain, resplendent in his top hat, red greatcoat, and cane, replied while continuing to scan the the edges of the forest. "They knew alright! Their scouts are always busy, but you never see them. Wait! There's a group coming now. Only about a dozen though. That's odd, but perhaps they are a delegation sent to invite us to their village."

The Indians did not look friendly. They drew up in what almost looked like a skirmish line, bows in hand. "See to your loads men," Lisa said quietly. "No women with them. Not a good sign. I hope those few braves are not foolish enough to try an attack. Bluefoot, signal the other boats to be ready."

"Captain suh, how about I go on ashore and do a little dancin' for 'em? Maybe cheer 'em up some."

"Good idea, Dancer King. Take Tom along with you. Try to find out where the rest of their people are. See if they've come to trade. Be careful."

Tom led the way. The Dancer followed, bowing, leaping, and twisting like a new-born buffalo calf.

The trappers relaxed somewhat, as it appeared that all was well ashore. The braves crowded around the laughing and cavorting black man until he was almost hidden from Lisa and his men.

Then it happened! Two braves grabbed Dancer's arms, pinning them back. He was thrown down and two more Indians fell across his body. Tom shouted angrily but was immediately knocked to his knees and kicked aside.

There was a rattling sound as a dozen trappers cocked and leveled their weapons. "Hold off you fools!" the Captain roared. "You might hit Tom or The Dancer!"

Relying on just that precaution, the Indians half dragged and half carried Dancer King into the forest. "Get ashore!" Lisa ordered, but the men had anticipated the order and were already racing down the gangplank. Lisa was about to follow when a small hand grabbed his coattails.

"Not go." Pumpkin said, holding on. "Not go!"

"Why not child? Your father needs help!"

"Not go. Daddy back dinner time."

"Listen to him, Captain. The boy know. He know here." Polly patted Pumpkin's small chest.

"The kid's likely right Captain," said John Colter, a man highly respected since he had been one of Lewis and Clark's soldiers on their first expedition. "They're probably planning to hold him for ransom. I think I might have seen that one who was doing the sign language with Tom Bluefoot. But it's funny, I don't think he was with the Arikara then."

"Horses! Bunch horses!" Pumpkin said, tugging on Lisa's coat again.

The Captain lifted the boy to his shoulder and whispered, "tell me!"

"There. Come over there." Pumpkin did not point, but looked intently to the north. "Want get down. Mama hold hand."

All were puzzled at the child's words. Every eye was fixed on the northern shore of the Missouri, until the first group of Indians suddenly re-appeared. Tom was limping back toward the boat but stopped when the speaker approached, followed by six others.

Colter quietly nudged Lisa's arm. "Want me to shoot that varmint?" he whispered.

"No John. They know we won't shoot while they've got Dancer. Tell the other men to hold off, but be ready."

Polly hurried to Lisa's side, pulling Pumpkin by the hand. "'Scuse! Scuse. Pumpkin keep saying horses come! He say 'four horns'."

Manuel Lisa heard her words, but never took his eyes off the scene developing in the clearing. Tom had let the Indians meet him and was once again attempting to use his poor sign language.

Despite the seriousness of the situation the Captain had to smile. He had been trying to teach the boy about time. The two of them had worked out a plan, using how long it would take to dink a full horn of water. If the boy's prediction of 'four horns' was right, more riders would reach them in less than five minutes.

"The boy may only be playing a little game with me, but signal the other boats to be ready. If more people <u>do</u> come they are probably the main force behind these who face us. <u>Tom</u>!" he shouted. "What do they want?"

"They've got Dancer hid back there somewhere. If we give them 'fire sticks', blankets, and some trade items they'll let him go. What should I tell them?"

"Tell those renegades that we will not negotiate at all until they bring Dancer King back where we can see him." Tom did a fair job of signing.

The Indian spokesman made a gesture back toward the forest. Immediately four more braves appeared. Dancer was not with them.

"Well that's still not all of the first bunch that showed up," Colter said quietly. "Do you think they're waiting for reinforcements?"

"Very likely. Tell the men to start moving supplies to the thwarts for a barricade. The Indian women should be ready to keep powder and lead coming to the men."

"They're gonna bring him out!" Bluefoot yelled.

Two braves dragged the black man into the open. All aboard were shocked at the sight. They had bound him hand and foot, as well as tied a choking rawhide noose around his neck. Worst of all however was the bloody scratches on his cheeks, arms, and shoulders.

"Those <u>devils</u>!" Captain Lisa growled. "They've already started to torture the man."

"Permission to open fire?" John Colter asked.

"No! They'll kill him and Tom too. <u>Tom</u> <u>Bluefoot</u>! Get back to the boat. <u>Hurry</u>! Colter, as soon as the interpreter is close enough to get aboard, give the order to . . ."

Lisa's words were cut off by the thunder of hooves and the war cries of many riders. They galloped into the clearing and quickly surrounded Dancer's kidnappers. The two men holding Dancer's bonds were tomahawked where they stood. The others tried to flee but arrows found nearly all before they could enter the forest.

All present on the keelboats were speechless with astonishment. The entire episode had lasted less than "two horns"!

The leader of the warriors reined his horse up to the boat, right hand high in the universal sign of peace. He wore a beautifully quilled shirt, carried a round buffalo shield, also adorned, and wore a magnificent eagle feather headdress.

Lisa grabbed his top hat, which had fallen in the excitement, and began buttoning his scarlet coat. Before he'd had time to compose himself the chief motioned for another mounted man to come forward.

"Salud, Anglaise!"

"Salud, young man!" Lisa boomed, thrilled that conversation would be much easier now. He turned to John. "Take two men and get Tom and Dancer King back on board. Keep a sharp eye out. These people seem friendly, but don't turn your back on them yet!"

Polly jumped forward, grabbed the sobbing Pumpkin's hand and ran down the gangplank to see her man. Colter and the others had already cut the thongs that were digging into his wrists and ankles. They led him down to the river where Polly began washing away the blood.

"Why did they hurt you like that Papa?" Pumpkin sobbed, still not sure that his father would be alright.

"Well boy," Dancer answered, trying to grin, "they was determined that I was a fake, and that I'd <u>painted</u> myself with something. They tried to scratch it off! Haw haw!"

The moment he heard his beloved French language, Phillipe ran forward to learn what was happening. He soon began loudly translating so the rest would also be informed of how this miracle had come upon them.

"Listen! Phillipe tell what is ze going on here," he cried. "Zese horsemen, zey are real southern Arikara. These others who took our Dancing man, zey are . . . what you call 'renegades'! Some Ponca, some Cheyenne. Zay were kicked out of their clans so now zey band together and rob and kill."

"About a dozen of 'em won't be robbin' anybody anymore! Haw haw!" one of the trappers put in. "I'll bet . . ."

"There is much more Phillippe tell you," he interrupted. "These good ones, tell us come to their town for trade and feasting. Ze Capitaine say we go there tomorrow. How you like what Phillipe say, eh? How you like?" Phillipe looked around abruptly. It appeared he had lost his audience. Most of the men from all three boats were crowding the gunwales to watch what few had seen, and none would ever forget.

Polly snatched little Pumpkin from his father's side and fairly dragged him away from the horror developing in the clearing. A crowd of mostly young Southern Arikara braves were "counting coup" on the bodies of dead renegades which lay scattered about in various forms of contortion. Their unearthly screams sent shivers up the spines of even the strongest hunters and trappers who were watching.

Scalps were taken first. A razor sharp flint knife circled the head. A quick jerk lifted the scalplock, as even more screams erupted. Since there were not enough scalps to go around, the Indians soon began to improvise, taking fingers, ears, and even teeth from the dead.

Of all those watching the grisly scene, Manuel Lisa was undoubtedly the most refined. Raised in the cosmopolitan city of New Orleans, he had enjoyed the mansions and genteel activities of the well-to-do citizens there. Still, he knew that he must, if not respect, at least tolerate the warriors' customs. Successful trade depended upon it.

"Go to the others and help with little Pumpkin. You should not see this," he told Forest Flower who was at his side. "It appears the lad is trying to get a look at this awful business. He is a fine, fine boy. Go now."

He turned to the scene again, keeping an impassive look on his face. In a way he could sympathize with the victorious Arikara. After all the same thing would be done to them should an enemy tribe attack their village.

As the true Arikara were leaving, Captain Lisa addressed his group. His remarks were most welcome even though Phillipe had already told them most of what had gone on and what was to come. "Fortunately for us, Northern Arikara scouts have been watching our progress for a least a week. They were also aware of those lurking brigands who tried to kidnap our Dancer. We will go to Chief Fox Taker's village tomorrow. They had been visited by the Rogers and Clark expedition some years ago, and are anxious to trade."

With the help of his daughter, Forest Flower,whom he still called "Cattail", Tom Bluefoot dragged himself aboard. He found a small cask and sank down upon it, rubbing a badly bruised elbow. "I'm getting too old for this kind of life," he told the girl. "Are you being treated well, my daughter?"

"Oh yes!" she gushed. "Mr. Lisa gives me the best of <u>everything</u>!" Her mother, Menseeta, had overheard. She sniffed angrily and turned away. Tom said nothing. Everything that mattered to him had already been said.

Chief Fox Taker's village was a welcome sight to all of Manuel Lisa's fellow traders. The homes were substantial and semi-permanent. Built over arching poles and packed with earth, they were warm in winter and cool in summer. The Arikara only left these dwellings for a few weeks in early fall for the annual buffalo hunt, which had been particularly successful this year.

"Well would you lookee here," Colter laughed. "Them two cousins must have finally figured out which end of the rifle does the shootin'!"

"'Even a blind hog kin root up a acorn onct in a while' my old Pappy used to say," a fellow trapper quipped as they watched Brady and Joe triumphantly enter the village, each loaded with a haunch of fresh venison. "Then agin', maybe that deer just surrendered to 'em. Haw haw."

"At least they didn't get lost this time. Well not that we <u>know</u> <u>of</u> anyway!"

Great quantities of food were being prepared as there were nearly two thousand Native Americans plus the fifty-two guests from Lisa's trading company. Especially appreciated by the traders was the corn, squash, beans, and other vegetables recently harvested from the Arikaras' large gardens. They were tired of a constant diet of only meat.

When at last all had eaten so much they could hardly stand it was time for speeches and dancing. As night fell the cooking fires were built up enough to light the entire central area.

"My friends," Lisa began, raising his top hat to rows and rows of seated Indians, "we of the great nation to the east thank you for your kindness." He waited while the young French-speaking brave translated, then continued. His words lasted nearly another "ten horns". He then indicated that Fox Taker come forward. With great ceremony he placed a gleaming silver crescent around the chief's neck. There was a cacophony of "oo- ooing", the Arikaras' version of applause.

Three minor headmen were also rewarded, then it was apparent to all that it was time for the dancing to begin. The "maiden dance" was first. Some forty or fifty young women, dressed in their finest, formed two concentric circles around the bonfire. The younger girls circled daintily around the older performers, dancing in the opposite direction.

"Man oh man!" Dancer King groaned. "They's 'spectin' me to put on a real good show for 'em and I cain't!"

"Is it your ankle, Husband?" Polly asked, continuing to apply bear grease to his upper body.

"Oh Polly, them savages as caught me had them thongs so tight it just natcherly cut the blood right off my old foots! This one," he pointed to his right foot, "ain't bad. But this one here is!"

"You'll have to do the best you can," Polly murmured, streaking his cheeks and chin with white paint from the trading stock. "The Captain expects you to do the dancing to get them all in a good mood for the trading."

"I knows. I knows. Just don't be flummoxed iffn I just falls right over though. Looks like the ladies is done so I reckon it's time for the Dancer King to kick up his heels fer this crowd. Wish I had my drum and headdress. Them rascals that caught me runned off with 'em."

Nearly twenty years in slavery had conditioned the big man to be ready and appear eager to please those who owned him, no matter what.

The present situation was actually little different.

With an ear-shattering yell he hopped into the firelight. Did anyone know he was in pain? Not likely! He did his dancing with such amazing enthusiasm that the "oo-ooing" began almost immediately. Hopping mainly on his right foot seemed to the watchers that he was doing a sort of special performance for them. When he finally finished, the onlookers rushed forward to touch him. Nearly all who did so immediately looked at their fingers. No, the color did not come off!

Dancer was not the first black man some of them had ever seen. York, William Clark's servant, had been with the expedition that had visited them several years before.

An absolutely remarkable man in many ways, York had been a slave for at least two generations of the Clark family. As often happened in slavery days, as a piece of "property" he was passed down to William Clark, co-leader of the 1803 – 1806 Expedition of Discovery.

Of fine physique and obvious intelligence, he had done much to ensure the eventual success of the mission. Unfortunately however, upon the corps' return he received little recognition for his contribution. Nearly every other member of Rogers' and Clark's corps was awarded, not only acclaim but even payment in the form of land grants.

York, who had been allowed considerable freedom and responsibility during the three year expedition, returned to find himself considered only a lowly slave once more!

By all accounts. including the actual journals kept by Rogers and Clark, York was a great favorite with the Native American women encountered on the journey. It was intimated that some of the women hoped to have children by the black man, believing that such offspring would be extraordinarily blessed in many ways.

In an attempt to acknowledge York's life after the expedition, researchers met with frustrating contradictions. Sources deemed reliable differ considerably regarding the man's final years. Clark himself claimed to have given York his freedom, but there is little credible evidence of this assertion. Even more intriguing is the documented report by Betts and Taure' that in the year 1834 they had encountered an African American man living with the Crow Indians. He had several wives,  was fluent in the language of the Crows, and appeared to be highly regarded by them. Furthermore the man asserted that he had first met this tribe when he had arrived with Lewis and Clark many years before!

Which version is the truth about York's years following the Lewis and Clark "Expedition of Discovery"? Perhaps it can ever be known.

Due to the flavor of the times, accounts about slaves, former slaves, and slave owners were often jaded, misrepresented, or simply untrue. This was also true to some extent about the American Indians.

Even the supposed year of York's death is unclear, but probably occurred in the late eighteen thirties. A statue meant to honor the famous black man has been erected near the Ohio River in Louisville, Kentucky, but since no photographs or other representations of him are known to exist, the sculptor's imagination had to serve.

Recently President William Clinton posthumously awarded York the rank of sergeant in the United States Army.

\*       \*       \*

Manuel Lisa's American Fur Company was enjoying much success. The natives were generally friendly and eager to acquire the items they were unable to make for themselves.

Kettles, needles, hatchets, clothing, and even some rudimentary farming equipment quickly replaced those which had served them for thousands of years. Most valued of course were the ornaments of silver, copper, or glass, which the Indians, both men and women, craved. Glass beads quickly replaced dyed and flattened porcupine quills for the enhancement of shirts, leggings, and moccasins.

The trading was going quite well. Fur-bearers were so plentiful now that teams of trappers were sent out along the creeks and rivers to trap the beaver, whose pelts were prized above all others. The men would often be gone for several days at a time, until the animals in that area were nearly depleted. They would then return to camp, laden with huge packs of raw and bloody skins.

As winter drew near, ice was closing the Missouri and the Platte. Lisa paid a few friendly Indians to guard the keelboats until he returned.

They bartered for horses and continued to the north and west, finally reaching Fort Raymond at the juncture of the Yellowstone and Bighorn Rivers. Lisa and an earlier crew had built the stockade several years before.

*        *        *

"But why <u>not</u>, Mama? I should tell him. I <u>know</u> it. I <u>do</u>!"

"There are some things, Pumpkin, that should <u>not</u> be told, even when we are sure of them. When you are older you will be better able to understand these things."

"But the sickness will take him! I know it in my head."

"I do not doubt you my son. I do not! But still . . . Oh, I cannot . . . I just . . ."

"I will go and tell my father. He will be the one to show me what is right to do. You are but a woman after all!"

Polly shook her head as she continued scraping down still another heavy pelt. "What am I to do with you, my son?" she sighed. "That you have 'the gift' cannot be denied, but with it must come much, <u>much</u> wisdom. How can I help you gain that? You are still only my little boy. Go to your father then. This thing is too much for me."

"I <u>will</u> go to him. Where is he?"

"He is with Captain Lisa. You must wait until they are done. Or at least beyond the Captain's hearing. Do not let our leader learn what you know. Do you <u>hear</u>?"

"Wait. Here comes my Papa now. And the  Captain has gone somewhere else. Papa, <u>Papa</u>! I want to talk to you."

"Not now Pumpkin. Polly, take the boy outside. What we must soon discuss is not for him to hear. What <u>is</u> it son? Stop pulling on my leggings. Your mother and I need to be alone right now."

Pumpkin's lower lip began to tremble. "I don't need to go outside of the tent, Papa. I already know what you and Mama will discuss. Those bad Indians are going to come at  us tomorrow. But that's not what I need to ask you about."

Dancer and Polly stared at their son in complete astonishment. More and more their chubby pumpkin-colored child was exhibiting an uncanny ability to predict the future. "How . . . how do you  . . . can you be absolutely sure . . . sure of this, my son?" Dancer choked out.

"Of course," the boy said with an impatient sigh.

Polly drew the child to her. "He has told me what he wants to ask you," she said, turning frightened eyes on her husband. "I think you should hear him."

"I know what you and Grandpa have been talking about . . ."

"Pumpkin, I've told you before, I don't think it is right for you to call our Captain 'Grandpa'."

"But he wants me to. He likes it. I do too. Anyway it's something about him that I want to talk to you about."

Polly and Dancer looked at each other in dismay. Finally Dancer nodded. He led the boy outside, away from the two Arikara women Lisa had hired to help prepare the furs. He couldn't be sure how much English they understood. "Ask me then," he said, frowning at the boy.

"Captain Grandpa is sick. Not like this," he pantomimed vomiting, "and not like this" he coughed twice. "Mama says it would be bad to tell him. <u>Is</u> it bad to tell?"

"I think he ought to know it."

"But he is not sick, Pumpkin. Several of the men and I have been talking with him all morning. He is fine."

"But Grandpa doesn't know he's got a problem. It's down here," he patted his belly. Inside of here. On <u>him</u> I mean, not on me. Should I tell him or not?"

Dancer looked out at the mountains surrounding Fort Raymond. "How do I answer this peculiar child I've fathered?" he asked himself silently.

"Father?"

"Very well my son. Your mother is right in this. Neither she nor I doubt your ability, but until the Captain himself feels the sickness you've seen in your mind it would only distract him and make him feel very sad. He thinks that 'bad Indians' will come against us. So right now . . ."

"I <u>know</u> they are coming, Papa. I told you that."

"Yes you did. But you must remember that Mr. Lisa has a wife."

"Two wives! And he wants Forest Flower for a wife <u>too</u>!"

"Yes. And he has children. He is missing them. Do you think you should burden the man further by telling him he has some kind of sickness? Especially now that there may be an attack?"

"No I won't tell him. May I attend the meetings when you and the men decide things about the 'bad Indians' ?"

"Have you 'seen' anything about that?" Dancer hissed, his face close to that of his son.

"No, but maybe I will. Papa, did you know that that Arikara woman's boy, he's ten winters, has two brown puppies? He said I could have one if I gave him two armbands. Can I?"

Dancer had to smile. "Go back to your mother," he told the boy, perplexed that his gifted son could instantly become no different from any other seven-year-old!


     *        *        *

Manuel Lisa worked as hard as any of the men as they hurriedly did all they could to strengthen the stockade. The years of neglect had taken their toll, and it was doubtful how safe Lisa's American Fur Company would be.

As often happened, Pumpkin had not 'seen' anything specific about the attack that was surely coming. There was nothing the boy could do to cause his visions to happen, and so far as Dancer and Polly knew, he never tried to.

As night fell, fires were built up to help them with their preparations. All the women, Polly included, had been taught how to load for the men. Even the seven still unsold "trade muskets" had been unpacked and made ready for use.

Ignoring his mother's words, Pumpkin ran about, watching all that went on. He kept one eye on the boy whose dog he craved. That ten-year-old was strutting about importantly, proud to be included as a "loader" for the men.

"I want a puppy," Pumpkin told him, "the one with the black spot."

"Don't bother me. Can't you see that I am in charge of the women who are to keep the guns loaded? Besides, I told you,'two armbands'. Do you have them?"

"No, not yet. But maybe . . ." the boy hurried away.

"Mama, see that boy over there? He's the one who has two puppies. He won't give me one unless I give him two armbands. Could you ask Grandpa Captain for them? Just the copper ones would probably be alright."

"No! I'm busy. Go to your sleeping robe like I told you."

"Mama!"

"What now? Must I use a switch on your behind?"

"Mama."

"What?"

"Mama if that boy should get killed by an arrow, could I have that puppy with the black spot on its side? See, that way I wouldn't have to give away any armbands. It . . ."

Polly's open hand slashing across her son's head sent him staggering. "I will not hear of such an evil thought. Go to bed!"

Pumpkin ran crying to his robe beside the cooking shed, having no idea what he had said that was so wrong.

\*          \*          \*

They came at dawn. Nearly sixty armed Indians painted for war. It appeared that there were several different tribes making up the attacking force, but the majority were Blackfoot.

"Why are them Blackfoot Injuns comin' at us like they are, Frenchie? We ain't done nothin' to 'em that I know of," one of the men asked, peering over the wall.

Phillipe ignored the nickname. Most of the men had begun calling him that. He didn't mind. "I tell you zey are mad at us because of zat man over dere," he nodded to his left.

"You mean John Colter? Why he's nothing but a big liar. Did you ever hear him tellin' about that one place he went to? He claimed he saw steam risin' out of the ground, some of it blowin' way up in the <u>air</u>. He said boilin' mud, spring water in the winter time too hot to drink! And on and on like that there. Just because he was with Lewis and Clark that time, he has to tell stuff like that. <u>Boilin'</u> <u>Mud!</u> Why nobody could believe anything like that . But I still don't see why them Blackfoot devils got a burr under their blanket on account of him."

"Capitaine Clark, he make Colter go all ze way down ze Yellowstone Rivaire to see if there be many castor down there. Phillipe, he would have told zat man not to go down there."

"Why Not?"

"Because if traders trap ze castor, zen Blackfoot, Crow, any Indians, not get ze trade goods. Phillipe he can see zat it make <u>trouble</u>! But zen, nobody listen to me . . ."

Phillipe broke off in mid-sentence when he saw the Captain hurrying back along the line of defenders. Lisa paid no attention to the trapper and the Frenchman, as he had many more important matters to think of. "Phillipe," he called, "Where is your daughter?"

"She is down at ze corner, Mon Capitaine."

"Send her to me immediately!" he hurried away.

"Aha!" Phillipe whispered. "Pretty soon he ask Phillipe for permission to marry Floret Flruer. So . . . I be in a good place with ze Capitaine, eh?"

Captain Lisa hurried along the line. "Colter!" he shouted. "I'm putting you in charge. Give any orders that you feel are appropriate."

"Thanks Captain," he replied, never taking his eyes off his rifle barrel.

"What are they waiting for?" Lisa asked, turning to Colter again.

"Well Captain, they're scarin' us. That's why. They want us to see what a big gang of 'em is out there. It's sure as salt a good move too! Another thing. They're showin' us that it's more than one tribe that's ready to fight."

"What's your advice?" Lisa asked. Like all good managers he was ready to seek help and counsel from any who could supply it.

"Whatever we decide it better be quick! The main chief out there probably won't be able to keep that bunch quiet much longer. So I think . . ."

"<u>Grandpa</u>! <u>Grandpa</u>!" Pumpkin had broken loose from his mother and was racing to Lisa's side.

"Get back to the shack!" the Captain ordered. "You have no business here. Go to your father. Dancer, see to your son!"

"Bad Indians <u>back</u> <u>there</u>!" the boy shouted pointing back toward the far wall.

"No. They're out there in front of us. Here, I'll lift you up so you can see over the wall. They're not back there."

"I think he's right, Captain. I seen a bunch of 'em sneakin' back into the trees. They're probably gonna try to get around the fort and hit us from behind! <u>Bless</u> <u>that</u> <u>kid</u>!"

"What's your advice John? Should we try to fire a volley over their heads?"

"Where's he at, Captain?" Dancer yelled. "I thought he was with you. Oh, there he is, down by the . . . Oh <u>no</u>! He's . . . Captain! <u>Captain</u>! He's climbin' over the wall! Them Injuns will get him sure! <u>Colter</u>! . . . Captain! . . . Somebody! Stop him! <u>Polly</u>, he's outside of the fort! White man's God, protect our child!"

"Look at that boy!" Lisa gasped. "He's walking right up to them. They'll shoot him full of arrows! Quick, Colter, get a flag of truce ready. Grab some trade goods! Move man! <u>Move</u>!"

"Too late Captain. They won't hurt him. Not yet anyway. They admire anybody who ain't afraid of 'em. They'll likely hold him for ransom though."

"Somebody <u>do</u> <u>something</u>!" Polly screeched, peering over the wall. "My son will be <u>butchered</u> by those savages!"

John Colter tied a rag on the end of a ramrod, straddled the top of the wall and waved it frantically. The Indians ignored the flag of truce, mainly because every one of them was watching the golden-skinned child before them.

"Forest Flower," Captain Lisa mouthed over his shoulder, "bring my red jacket and top hat. Be quick! Colter, set four men at the gate. Dancer, Polly, Bluefoot, we're going out!"

As the heavy stockade gate creaked open a low growl could be heard from the attackers' ranks. Colter, the flag of truce held high, led Lisa, Dancer King, Polly, and Forest Flower into the open.

Five Crow Indians, the ones Pumpkin had "seen" behind the fort now appeared, bows drawn. They took up position behind the advancing "peace negotiators". Polly, ignoring them, suddenly broke free from her husband and raced to her child's side.

"No my mother," Pumpkin said, wriggling free of his mother's embrace. "Tell John and Tom Bluefoot to come to me. They will talk with their hands to these bad Indians."

Neither Lisa nor Colter in all their adventures had ever witnessed a stranger sight.

The only person present who was not shaking was Pumpkin.

"What do you want me to tell them, boy?" John Colter asked, peering in extreme consternation at the lad.

"Tell them that if they don't hurt any of us, you know, Papa, Mama, Tom, Captain Grandpa, you, that pretty Forest Flower,or me either, I can tell them things that will happen to them some time. Can you tell them all of that with your hands?"

The others formed a protective ring around the boy as Tom Bluefoot and John Colter approached the Blackfoot war chief and began signing.

The painted leader showed no indication that he understood. When Colter tried again the chief made a slashing motion with his left hand. Tom shook his head.

"He don't believe that you've got that there kind of power. I did all I could."

"I didn't think he would," Pumpkin said. "He looks like he's pretty dumb in his head. Well then I'll show him!"

Polly suddenly stepped up, her right arm circling her son's small body. "Tell them they can have all our trade goods. They can even have our salted pelts if they don't hurt the boy or attack us. Tell them John! Tom, tell them! Hurry!"

Dancer King stepped to her side in support.

"I'll show them now." Pumpkin said calmly. Mama, Papa, help me find a whole lot of little stones. Little enough for the 'hand game'."

As they quickly searched for the stones Pumpkin wanted, Colter signed that there would be a game of "hands". This was met by a shout of protest from the attackers. Several made the sign for anger at the delay.

Pumpkin stepped boldly forward and held out four pebbles. The chief snatched them away in disgust. Pumpkin pantomimed that the Blackfoot should begin the game, but the man merely spoke rapidly to those nearby.

At last he complied. The Indians were completely enthralled by this, the strangest thing any of them had ever seen. For the present an attack was postponed.

Hands behind his back, the chief waited a moment then thrust both closed fists in Pumpkin's face. Without a moment's hesitation the boy tapped the right hand. None were impressed. It was merely a lucky guess. Their expressions began to waver however, when Pumpkin chose correctly on five successive tries.

It was then that the child did something that completely convinced them all, attackers and traders alike. He stepped lightly along the line of closest braves, handing each some of the small pebbles that had been gathered up. Intrigued in spite of themselves most of them went along with the game. Now laughing aloud he skipped back along the line and pointed to each in turn. This time however, he not only correctly chose which hand held the stones, but using his chubby fingers, indicated how many tiny stones were hidden in each closed fist!

Still under the flag of truce, which for the moment the hostiles seemed to be honoring, the delegation re-entered the fort. No one knew what would happen next, but the Indians could be seen in heated discussion at the edge of the clearing.

Captain Lisa dropped to one knee and took Pumpkin's hand in his. "You may have not only saved our remaining trade goods and furs, but our lives as well! How can we thank you?

"We should pack up and leave!" Menseeta cried, holding her daughter, Forest Flower's, hand. Polly was nodding vigorously.

John Colter, still carrying the improvised "white flag" literally pulled Lisa to his feet. "We got to move fast, Captain. Them Crows and Blackfoots won't wait long."

"Right! Let's get back out there John. Maybe we can bargain with them. Come on."

Colter, Tom, Dancer, and Manuel Lisa ran from the fort again. The Blackfoot chief charged forward to meet them. Tom and Colter both desperately made the sign for a parlay. The chief signed back in a fury. Even those not skillful in the universal sign language of the plains had no doubt about what the Indians wanted.

"Is it what I think it is?" Lisa whispered.

"Yes, Captain. They'll let us alone if we hand over little Pumpkin and . . . and . . ."

"Well, what else?" the Captain hissed.

"They want Pumpkin and . . . and the girl you call Forest Flower."

"Never!" Lisa snarled.

"Beggin' yer pardon Captain, but they got us in a bad fix. They'll use fire arrows, burn the fort, kill all that's fit, and grab the boy and the girl anyway!"

"We can fight! We've got guns and they don't. Tell the men to be ready to fire at my command."

He never gave the order. Pumpkin came running from the fort, pulling Forest Flower by the hand. Before Dancer could grab his son the boy raced up to the chief and took hold of the Indian's hand. Forest Flower, terrified, stood there trembling, not knowing what to do. The decision was made for her when a young Blackfoot brave who had stayed close to the chief walked out and clamped a hand on her wrist.

"No!" Tom Bluefoot screamed. "She is <u>my</u> <u>daughter</u>!"

The warrior, still holding onto the girl, laughed in derision at the skinny, crippled Wyandot who confronted him. Without releasing the girl he raised his lance and cocked his arm. In another second he would have impaled Tom Bluefoot, but the chief stepped forward and pushed the lance down, signing rapidly as he did so. The young brave was his son.

"He's ordering a fair fight for the girl," John said, running up to Tom's side. "You'll have to fight him. Here's my knife. Don't let him get close to ya!"

Tom felt little fear. The position in which he found himself was eerily like the similar one some seven month ago. As before he remembered old Black Pipe's admonition; 'when death is inevitable face it with courage'."

But <u>was</u> death inevitable this time? He glanced at forest Flower, whom he would always think of as "Cattail". He tried to smile at the terrified girl but wasn't very successful at it.

The Blackfoot chief turned to his Indian allies and spoke so rapidly that John Colter could only catch a little of the meaning.

"What is it, John?" Captain Lisa whispered.

"It's as I thought. That young Blackfoot wants Forest Flower for his wife. It 'pears like he's big in the tribe. Might even be the Chief's son or something."

"He can't have her," Lisa growled.

"That ain't all Captain," Tom said. "They want the boy too."

"Little Pumpkin? What in the world do they want <u>him</u> for?"

"Think of it," John whispered. "They've seen how the kid can 'see things'. That would help 'em in war, help 'em when they gamble . . . who knows what else?"

"Should we . . ." Lisa's question stopped in mid-sentence, his mouth falling open in surprise as Pumpkin stepped up to Tom Bluefoot, took the knife and handed it back to John Colter.

"Grandpa Captain, I will go with them. The pretty girl too. We will be well. I have <u>seen</u> <u>things</u> that will happen many . . . many . . . a long time from now."

"Pumpkin, <u>no</u>! We can fight them. You don't need to do this!"

The boy turned to his father, tears flowing freely down his cheeks. "You have told me Papa," he said, " that it is usually best to do what is best for the <u>most</u>. I am not afraid. This way the fort will not be all burned down, and . . . and all the . . . <u>terrible</u> things I saw in my head won't happen."

Dancer fell to his knees and clasped his son in a desperate embrace, crying openly. "Are you sure, my son? Are you <u>very</u> <u>very</u> sure?" he choked out.

"Yes, Papa and Mama. I am sure. I will miss you and Mama and even Beth's girls too." He walked quickly to the awe-struck Indians, took Forest Flower's hand  and the two of them disappeared behind the attackers' ranks.

A terrible shriek split the air. Tearing at her hair with one hand, Polly dashed out of the fort and into the ranks. In her right arm was a wriggling brown puppy, the one with the black spot.

\*          \*          \*

Manuel Lisa's American Fur Company was forced to leave two days later.

Pumpkin's prediction that Lisa would have to return "before he wanted to" was fulfilled to the letter. What Pumpkin had known about the expedition leader's illness and had been discouraged from disclosing, also proved eerily accurate, as Lisa died of "unknown causes" [possibly cancer] some time after the expedition arrived back in St. Louis.

That Manuel Lisa had truly loved Tom Bluefoot's daughter, whom he had re-named Forest Flower, cannot be doubted. Possibly in respect to his Indian wife Mittain, the Omaha chief's daughter, and their two children, he had never violated the young woman.

It would be impossible to choose which mother's grief was the greater; that of Menseeta or Polly. Even though the son and the daughter were not dead at the time, both women knew that it was unlikely that they would ever see either one again.

Simon, who had become known as Dancer King and his first wife, Polly, eventually joined with Beth and the other Kickapoos who, thanks to Manuel Lisa's generosity, had arrived back in St. Louis eight months before.

Shortly after Simon's sad and discouraged followers were able to achieve a semblance of organization, a wealthy widower arranged for them to settle on a large tract of land in what would one day be called Oklahoma.

So after some trouble with local homesteaders, Simon was finally able to complete his assigned task of finding land on which a few more Kickapoos could settle "beyond where white people would ever come".

Other than the generous gift by the St. Louis lady, Simon was never acknowledged for the unusual but vital part he had played in helping to open the Northwest to trade and friendly relations with the indigent population there.

Toom-She-chi-Kwa ["Tom Bluefoot"] did not survive the return trip. He died in Menseeta's arms after nearly a week of severe lung problems. As food and other necessities were becoming critically low they had to hurry. He was buried in an unmarked grave on the riverbank near the site of present day Omaha, Nebraska.

Cattail [Forest flower] so far as is known, was treated reasonably well by her Blackfoot husband, but died at the age of thirty-two, having been exposed to smallpox, probably from fur trappers who had set up camp in Blackfoot territory.

Of Phillipe and Menseeta nothing is known, but there is some credible speculation that her son, Red Gopher, became a ranch hand, and was living in Canada.

As might be expected, Ripe Pumpkin's activities are well documented . The Crow nation, as well as the Blackfoot became very fond of him. He was afforded all sorts of privileges which made for a mostly enjoyable life.

The advantages Pumpkin was able to give to his adopted tribe was short-lived however. As could be expected, visiting gamblers quickly refused to play unless Pumpkin remained outside of the lodge!

His "gift" had helped his people win two small battles, and even better, avoid four more. But by his late twenties he had made it known that his powers were fading. This may be true, but what is more likely is that he was burdened by his ability to sometimes know what was going to happen. Certainly he recalled the good advice given him by his parents, Dancer and Polly, regarding how much anyone should be told about what the future held.

In later years Pumpkin, who now called himself Victory [or Victor] by both Native Americans and settlers, was asked to take part in a delegation to Washington, D.C. While there in 1834, he met with President Andrew Jackson, who was greatly impressed by the young man of Negro and American Indian descent. This was ironic in view of Jackson's well known position regarding the fate of the American Indians. This was proven by his signing into law of the "Indian Removal Act" in 1830, and his adamant support for the continuation of slavery in America.

Several area newspapers, most notably the Washington D.C. *Weekly Reporter,* covered Victor's efforts on behalf of his people. Many promises were made but little was actually accomplished. Welfare of Native Americans was not a priority with the United States Government at that time!

After a search of nearly six years, Pumpkin [Victor] finally located the run-down village of Pathways, founded by his father in the northeast corner of what was then Oklahoma Territory, near present day New Hope.

As he had expected, only some forty Kickapoos still lived there. All of his family had passed away except Beth's two daughters, neither of whom had ever married.

A nearby rancher, Alden Higgs, over the years had done his best to help the struggling Indians. He'd always been impressed by Simon, "The Dancer", who had never been re-captured by his former owners.

Some time after Simon's death at the age of fifty-six, Alden petitioned the commissioners of New Hope to pay for a small memorial stone in honor of the deceased ex-slave. Outraged at such a request for a <u>Negro</u>, they refused. Nonplussed, Higgs scratched the name and age  on a thin pine board and used it to mark the grave.

The ground being hard and stony, he finally simply secured the marker in a pile of rocks.

In the summer of 1950, a team of archaeological students from Oklahoma Methodist University attempted to find the grave site. A scattered pile of stones was located, but the wooden marker was long gone, a victim of the elements.

\*           \*           \*

## SO ENDS THE FINAL EPISODE IN THE "TOM BLUEFOOT TRILOGY"

Lloyd Harnishfeger, Pandora,Ohio, December, 2018

Printed in the United States
By Bookmasters